KATE GILMORE

Remembrance of the Sun

Houghton Mifflin Company
Boston 1986

Library of Congress Cataloging-in-Publication Data

Gilmore, Kate.
Remembrance of the sun.

Summary: Jill, an American high school student
living in Tehran, finds herself falling in love with an
Iranian rebel just at the time when the shah's
repressive treatment of his people is making violent
revolution inevitable.
1. Iran — History — Mohammed Reza Pahlavi, 1941–1979 —
Juvenile fiction. [1. Iran — History — Mohammed Reza
Pahlavi, 1941–1979 — Fiction] I. Title.
PZ7.G4374Re 1986 [Fic] 86-15393
ISBN 0-395-41104-1

Printed in the United States of America

P 10 9 8 7 6 5 4 3 2 1

for Mehdi Gangineh

Prologue

"Round her neck she wore a yellow rib-
bon. She wore it in the springtime and in the month of
May . . ." The old song goes round and round in my head as
I walk through the small New England town. They are wear-
ing yellow ribbons here for the American hostages in Iran.
The sweet old lady who is postmistress has one in her hair.
"They should bomb those dirty Iranians into the ground,"
she says to someone as I turn empty-handed from the mail-
box. "NUKE IRAN" is written in crude letters on the side of
Bill's Garage across the street.

"She wore it in the springtime . . ."

"Think Mozart," I tell myself sternly, but you know how
it is with certain songs. They're like the hiccups: the more
you try to shake them off, the tighter they hang on. It was
May when we parted under the flowering trees in the hills
above Tehran, but it is not for Shaheen that the yellow ribbons blossom in the gray town, not for my "lover who is far,
far away."

I leave the angry village and walk out along the fog-bound
cliffs. My ribbon should be red, I think — red for revolution,
red for the blood of martyrs. Why doesn't he write? I try not
to think of the possible answers.

It is good to be alone again out here where the drifting fog covers the familiar world and the voice of the invisible sea mumbles on the dark rocks below my path. Here my eyes can turn inward to gaze at pictures cut like diamonds in my memory, pictures that blaze with the hard brilliance of a desert sun and never seem to fade.

I see a street of dusty plane trees and the white skeletons of unfinished apartment towers rising among mud-brick walls. I see jeweled mounds of fruit spilling into the light from the black shade of awnings around the bazaar and a jagged mountain pass etched against the fabled Persian sky.

Two years have passed, an eternity of waiting, but in my memory it is all as fresh as yesterday. I would go back tomorrow if I could turn back the clock of history even to those last frightening weeks — back to the ugly, teeming, much loved city sprawling beneath its crown of mountain peaks.

I see myself in the car, always in the car beside Shaheen. Now we are skimming through the brown dunes at dusk with the lights of East Tehran twinkling in a bowl of darkness below and the high peaks still catching the last glow of setting sun. We are silent with the stillness of an old companionship while from the radio the urgent thrumming of the *tar* weaves in the desert twilight its ancient patterns of denial and desire.

Or we are caught in a hopeless traffic jam up in the hills of Shemiran. We are relaxed, joking about the shah, who has caused this mess by deciding to go out for once by car instead of helicopter. Shaheen, like so many Iranian students, is determined to get rid of the King of Kings, but for the moment he is good-natured about our plight. This ostentatious motorcade, which will tie up the streets for miles around, has given us yet more time to be together.

Again I see us as we climb alone in the bright, still air, up through the pinnacled rocks to the seven ice-green pools of Haft Hoz, or to the tea house in Pas Qaleh, high above the smoky streets of the city.

Or it is night in the narrow lanes of South Tehran. The fires of No Ruz are leaping against the walls, and everyone is jumping over them to bring good luck in the coming year.

That year brought no luck, although it did bring down the shah. It saw an end to a vast system of tyranny and the birth of a new one which was more evil than the old. For a moment the bright banners of freedom flashed in the Iranian sun, only to be swallowed once more by the dark. And in this dark Shaheen and his friends fight on, or at least I pray that they do, for if not, I cannot bear to think where they may be. The enemy has changed, and the conflict now seems endless.

For myself it is clear, I must do something besides wait and dream of times which will not come again. My memories are almost all of happiness, so let me capture them. Let me cast out a net of words into the receding tide of the past and pull it in full of things that shine and leap with joy.

Chapter 1

It took the four of us in our family about three months to become adjusted to Tehran. Anyone who has tried it will agree that this is a testament to our flexibility. We arrived in the full heat of summer, dazed by twelve hours in a packed jumbo jet, slightly discouraged by the studied surliness of Iranian stewardesses, but still bemused by visions of nightingales and roses.

"What became of the mountains?" my mother asked as we waited on the scorching pavement outside Mehrabad Airport for a driver from the oil company to pick us up.

It was a reasonable question. Tehran is right on the lap of one of the world's great mountain ranges. We had seen them from the plane — mile upon mile of savagely beautiful, barren peaks. Now they had unaccountably disappeared.

"Over there?" I said, pointing to a line of shadowy gray forms just barely visible to our left. "The air seems just a bit thick today."

"Someone told me that the sky here is the loveliest shade of blue," she continued. "I was looking forward to that."

"It looks repulsive," my brother, James, said. "I hope I

can find plenty of good books, because I'm sure not going to spend much time out of doors."

"You know better than to judge a place from its airport," my father said. "Any minute now we will be whisked away to scenes of unimaginable luxury, by which I mean showers, beds, and food that has been spread out on a table with at least an inch between dishes. This should change our whole outlook on Tehran."

If someday my father arrives in a place which is ghastly enough to dim his optimism, I hope to have had enough sense to stay at home. Our driver finally arrived, but to say that we were whisked away would give an entirely false impression of what it was like to move around Tehran. During the interminable ride from the airport, we continued to look for signs of Middle Eastern splendor. There, after a few miles, was the huge monument the shah had built to be the gateway to the city. It was, in fact, very impressive, though silhouetted against a background of smog, and the greensward at its feet was filled with a profusion of roses. After the monument there were more flat miles of double highway lined with low brown buildings, punctuated here and there by clusters of new white buildings in various stages of completion or abandonment.

The traffic worsened as we approached the city, and soon our progress was reduced to a crawl. The sidewalks were crowded with women draped from head to foot in voluminous black *chadors*. I found the combination of gray air, brown buildings, and black-robed women not at all encouraging.

When we arrived at the Park Hotel in downtown Tehran, we found that reservations had not been made for us, and there was no room. Phone calls were made, rather reluctantly I thought, which resulted in our being bundled back into the car for another endless ride to the Hilton on the northern edge of town. There, wrapped in the bland comforts of a huge international hotel, we gradually recovered from the journey and began to contemplate the city which was to be our home.

My father is an oil engineer, and we are experienced wanderers. Strangely enough, however, we had so far been spared the Middle East, and nothing had prepared us for the complications of beginning a new life in Tehran. I will not dwell on the grisly details of looking for a house and the things to put in it. Tehran was vast, hot, confusing, and while people like hotel desk clerks spoke English, many equally important people like taxi drivers did not. We had studied Farsi a bit before we came, but could neither make ourselves understood nor understand one word that was said to us.

We were saved from total despair by finding a house fairly promptly. High in the foothills of Shemiran, above the heat and smog of the central city, it had huge, cool rooms and a tiny garden, most of which was taken up by a swimming pool. The fact that the rent was about twice what we could afford scarcely dampened our enthusiasm. We are not a family much given to financial anxiety.

There remained the problems of daily life — those purchases, for example, which at home are so simple as to be made almost unconsciously. Who chronicles the drama of buying a can opener in Boston? But in Tehran it can be a major event. Still, each small victory made the next battle seem less alarming. Day after day we reached out into the forbidding complexity of Tehran, and day after day it became less strange. By the time school opened in the fall, our new city had begun to seem like home.

Chapter 2

*As the daughter of a much traveled con-*sultant, I have mixed feelings about new schools. There is a bit of ho-hum-here-we-go-again and a lot of genuine excitement. Like my father, I am an optimist, always ready to believe that somewhere in the swirling confusion of a brand-new school may be hidden something or someone really wonderful.

Although very large, Tehran Community School was easy to adjust to because two thirds of the students were also wanderers from all over the world. Few had been long in Tehran, and many were as newly arrived as we were. The other third were Iranians who were supposed to feel privileged to be mingling with all of us fascinating foreigners. Most of them, in fact, felt that it was the other way around. But no matter. It was a stimulating place, and in it I found Shaheen.

This is not to say that Shaheen was a hidden treasure in my new school. He played first French horn (or "principal horn" as these exalted creatures prefer to call themselves) in the Community School band, and being a horn player myself, I could scarcely miss him. I went in to band the first day with the usual mixture of excitement and apprehension,

4

and there he was, back row center, unmistakably first horn, unmistakably superior. Oblivious of the awful din as fifty-odd amateur wind players warmed up, he seemed to sit in his own little well of silence — a slender figure at ease in his chair, the intricate, gleaming coils of a big double horn lying negligently in his lap. The dark eyes under straight, thick brows brooded on some distant view and did not noticeably brighten at the sight of an American girl approaching with a horn under her arm.

Travel and hotel living had done nothing for my playing, and at the beginning of school I was given the unenviable part of fourth horn. From fourth I rapidly rose to third, and there I stuck, one chair away from the object of my admiration, playing my heart out and hoping to be noticed. The second was a German boy named Helmut, a solid, dependable player. He was also a rather large person, and it seemed to me that Shaheen seldom craned his neck to see what I was doing, wearing, or thinking. The two of them talked horn-player talk in the pauses between pieces and also before and after rehearsal.

Things took a sudden turn for the better on the day that the Empress Farah came to our school. The reason for this somewhat strange event is that the low, rambling school buildings had once been a hospital, and in that hospital, some forty years earlier, the empress of Iran had been born. Farah in those days seemed actually to enjoy her public relations chores, and the Tehran papers were always full of pictures which showed her kneading bread in remote villages or chatting cozily with wild-looking tribesmen on the oil rigs. So a state visit to her birthplace was all in a day's work.

It was a hot September day when we all turned out on the playing field to greet the queen. I was pleased to see that a small stand had been built for the band. We would have a terrific view of everything and maybe even a touch of breeze from time to time. I scrambled up over the edge of the platform and then stopped dead in my tracks. There was the last row as usual — the snare drum, the bass drum, the triangle, the tympany and the tympanist bent over them in his classic listening pose; there was poor Dorothy in the last chair of the horn section; and there was my chair and also Helmut's, and both were empty. My heart was doing peculiar things in my chest, and I felt extremely short of breath. "You'll never be able to play, you stupid girl," I said to myself as I looked beyond the gap at Shaheen. He was gazing at me haughtily and, I thought, rather disapprovingly down his long Iranian nose.

"What happened to Helmut?" I asked of no one in particular.

"He caught a fly ball with his mouth," someone reported with a tasteless giggle.

"That's not funny," I said, cringing at the thought. "I suppose I should play second?" My tone of total cool wouldn't have fooled a six-year-old.

"Well, someone had better, and you're the only other horn player I see for miles around," Shaheen said, and Dorothy never even cringed. Such is the life of the fourth horn.

I moved over next to him feeling somewhat less than welcome and glanced up at Mr. Perenyi, our conductor, to see if he cared where I sat. He gave me a friendly but absent-minded wave from the podium, and I concluded that the internal affairs of the horn section were about the last thing on his mind. Mr. Perenyi was a Hungarian and a formidable musician. How he came to be conducting a high school band in Tehran was one of those mysteries which abound in foreign colonies. He was also a very nice man and a great admirer of the first horn he had been lucky enough to acquire. Shaheen could do as he wished with his section.

"All right, Jill, think you can cope?" he asked me as I started to arrange the music.

"The day I can't play any part of 'Shah-an-Shahi' is the last day I play at all," I said, hiding under mild indignation the pleasure I felt at hearing him speak my name.

He smiled then, and the quick, transforming smile impaled me where I sat. "Too right, I'm afraid. It is a bit simple-minded, but then, most national anthems are."

"I think 'The Star-Spangled Banner' offers a wisp of challenge," I said, "but perhaps only to singers. Would you believe I've never played it?"

He looked at me incredulously. "You did play in a band in the States?"

"Third horn. It's my specialty."

"And you never —"

"Well, we never had an occasion during the one year I was there. I'm sure it would have come up before I graduated," I said consolingly. He seemed to be taking it much to heart.

"This must be one of the wonders of democracy — not having to play the bloody anthem all the time," Shaheen said.

"I hadn't thought about it."

"No, you wouldn't," he shot back. "You take liberty for granted."

I glanced around uneasily at the four impassive security men who were standing around the band, ready presumably to tackle any musician who might be thinking of shooting poison darts out of his instrument. I might take liberty for granted at home, but I certainly didn't here — not after having my horn case searched when I came into school this morning and my peanut butter sandwich confiscated. Anything in a paper bag had acquired an ominous significance on this day of days. It also seemed like a poor time to discuss the pleasures of democracy, but the security men remained impassive, and Shaheen appeared to have dropped the conversation altogether. Probably I had impressed him as too witless to live. He was staring disdainfully into the murky distance, his shining horn on his lap, his long fingers playing absently with the keys.

I studied his profile surreptitiously. He had the national nose all right and a dense, black mustache, but the rest of his face didn't recede from these dominant features as was so often the case among Iranian boys. The rest of his face was very satisfactory indeed. In fact, the rest of Shaheen was entirely satisfactory. I had never fancied the football-player type, and he was lightly built but broad shouldered and a bit over average height. He carried himself with a slightly arrogant poise which must have put some people off, but I found it hopelessly attractive.

Farah was late. This surprised no one; still it was hot, and our eyes were strained from squinting into the blinding brightness of the smog in search of the royal vehicle.

Suddenly someone pointed and silence fell as we listened to the clatter of helicopter blades coming in through the shimmering air over the playing fields. A lone machine appeared and made a circle over our heads before turning away again to the north. The student body moaned in unison.

"That was the decoy," Shaheen said. "If someone wants to waste ammunition on that one, our lady will simply fly back to the palace, and some dumb pilot will have had the privilege of dying for queen and country — unless they miss, which is more than likely."

This time I was really alarmed. "Shaheen," I hissed, "one of the pigs is looking at us."

"One of the what?" he asked with a startled glance.

"Oh, sorry," I said. "I guess that's not the best choice of word in this country, even for the police."

"No, no, I like it," he said and proceeded to try it out in Farsi — "*khook, khook.*" It began with a harsh, aspirated sound which made the word sound even uglier than it did in English.

"Please be careful," I begged. "I'm not up to playing first horn, at least not in the concert."

"Don't worry," he said. "They don't know what we're talking about, and you are not going to get a chance at my place. What would Helmut say?"

"Helmut is going to be out of the running for a long, long time," I said cheerfully. "Poor baby."

"And you are going to be practicing very hard," was the discouraging answer. "Lots of repulsive scales in the lowest possible register, if you want to play second."

"I don't, or maybe, on second thought, I do," I added, remembering that playing second meant sitting next to Shaheen. "Anyway, I will, so don't worry. The low practice will probably be good for me."

"This I can promise," he said. "How much do you practice, by the way?"

"An hour a day," I said, stretching a point.

"Not enough. Two is the absolute minimum, if you want to get anywhere."

"But all that stupid homework," I wailed, "and that endless bus ride."

"Be glad you don't have to take Persian studies."

I was properly abashed. In addition to the regular courses

that everybody had to take, the Iranian students had several hours a day (presumably at night) of work in their own language and culture. These courses were reputed to be ghastly. If besides all this Shaheen practiced several hours a day, it was an impressive work load.

"Do you want to be a professional?" I asked.

Shaheen gazed off into the white sky toward the mountains hidden in the city's perpetual haze, toward the palaces on the cool hillsides in the north. "That depends," he said softly. "That depends greatly on what happens here in the next year."

I felt a quiver in the pit of my stomach. "What do you mean?" I whispered. "Is something going to happen in the next year?"

Now, however, it was his turn to be cautious. "Almost certainly not," he said brusquely and turned to studying the music on his stand.

I saw that he had covered the Iranian national anthem with a copy of the Strauss First Horn Concerto — a bit of one-upmanship if there ever was one. I rather hoped that he couldn't really play this beautiful and hideously difficult piece but feared that he could.

"Can you play it?" I asked brazenly.

"All of it? Straight through? What a hope," Shaheen said, "but I'm working on it."

I pointed to a high B-flat in the first movement, a note to which I was only beginning to aspire, if that's the word for it, but Shaheen shrugged. "B-flat's no problem," he said, "although playing it that soft is not easy. I have a natural upper register; it's something you're born with."

"That's not true," I cried. "Or at least it's not fair if it is true."

He grinned. "All it takes for the rest of you is work, work, work," he said, and I made a terrible face. "Anyway," he went on, "I told you I couldn't play it all the way through. It's horribly grueling, and the final presto is just too damn fast, so there; you can stop eating your heart out."

"Who said I was eating my heart out?" I was determined not to show too much abject admiration but still wishing this bizarre flirtation would go on forever. It was so amazing to be actually talking to Shaheen after weeks of silent hopefulness.

Unfortunately, whatever he might have said next was drowned by the arrival of Farah's helicopter. The rest of the student body (less happily occupied than I) must have been almost too hot and tired to care, but still the national anthem sounded fine as it was sung in Farsi by the entire school right down through kindergarten. I stood in a daze of heat and happiness as the empress gave her gracious little speech, waved to the applauding throng, and climbed back into her helicopter. If someone had asked me five minutes later, I couldn't have repeated one word she had said nor described one item of her doubtless beautiful costume.

Now, of course, everything went to pieces. I was almost knocked off the back of the bandstand in the general stampede, and when I next looked around for Shaheen, he was gone without a trace. For a time confusion reigned as we headed for classrooms which were spread around the huge compound. Those of us who had been so unwise as to bring lunches in paper bags made a gloomy detour by the kiosk, where such delights as warm yogurt drink flavored with rose water were offered to sustain the desperate. A few even managed to get out the front gate and duck into the corner store for a Mars bar or a Kit Kat.

11

I drank my yogurt thing in one courageous draft. It was, at least, nourishing, and by the time the bus left my stomach would have settled. Then I could sit dreamily through the traffic jams absorbed in a new set of fantasies until I reached my bare, breezy home in the hills.

Chapter 3

As usual, the bus driver dropped James and me three blocks down the hill from our side street. Even with books and a French horn to carry, I still enjoyed the brief walk. I liked peering into the walled gardens of the fanciful and luxurious villas that climbed the steep slopes of Shemiran, and we both liked hopping back and forth over the *jube* which here, so high in the hills, was always full of sparkling fresh water. These irrigation ditches were everywhere in Tehran. They ran on either side of nearly every street, bringing the abundant water of the mountains to all parts of the city.

Today my brother seemed subdued, and I searched my repertoire for something that would cheer by infuriating.

"James and Jill went up the hill . . ." I ventured.

"Stop it, you abominable person," James said.

"You don't like nursery rhymes any more?"

"Only in a historical context," my brother replied.

James was eleven, brilliant in an erratic way, and very good at a number of things, few of which were featured at Community School. He was one of a very small number of people with whom I cared to spend any extended period of time.

We continued to climb in amiable silence while I enjoyed the outer view and James contemplated some even more exotic inner landscape. To my right, across a vacant lot full of building materials, garbage, and half-wild dogs, the flanks of the Alborz mountains descended into the last straggle of luxury homes. The barren slopes were rose and ochre in the late afternoon light except where, here and there, a line of dusty green traced the course of a stream in the foothills. I sighed.

"I want to climb up there, Jamie," I said. "I want to so much it makes my bones ache."

"So climb," he said. "You won't have to worry about getting lost. The mountains are up and home is down. What could be simpler?"

"I don't know. For some reason I'm scared to start. They look so lonely."

"You're dippy," James said, but I knew it would be useless to ask him to come with me. I might not be much of an athlete, but compared to James my interest in sports was positively Olympic. He was an interior person.

We turned off the steep slope of Asef into a gravel road lined with modest new houses, then left again onto the even more primitive surface of Kuche Jilá, half a block of rutted dust with our house at the bottom.

Our mother was in the kitchen watching the houseboy wash the floor and wringing her hands. Ali had his trousers rolled up and was wading around enthusiastically, ankle deep in water, making wild swishing motions with the mop.

"Will one of you children please tell him not to use so much water," Mum said. "I can't stand it. This place is a swamp. How am I supposed to get dinner? You'll need life preservers to get a glass of milk."

"Ali!" James shouted. "*Ziad ab. Kheili ziad ab.*"

"I can get that far," she said indignantly. "'Too much water' simply does not convey enough to this person."

Ali was, as always, delighted to see James, the little master. "Hey, Jamie," he cried. "I am water good."

"Not that," my mother wailed. "Not Ali-English. Not now."

"Ali," I said slowly, marshaling my limited but growing Farsi into what I hoped was a reasonable argument. "My mother does not like so much water on the floor, and it is not necessary. In America where there is much water, we wash the floor with very little. It works well, and when you are finished, you can go into the kitchen."

Ali was not convinced, but he did switch to his native language. "Tehran has much water," he said. "Why not use it?"

The water was now ebbing sluggishly out through the drain in the kitchen floor, leaving behind muddy streaks at which Ali swiped in a halfhearted fashion. The fun was over now, and the delight of the desert dweller in the prodigal use of water had been spoiled by these inconsiderate if usually agreeable foreigners.

After a moment, however, he brightened. "Missus!" he cried, switching back to his version of our language. "I am Tajrish egg?"

"No, Ali, you are not a Tajrish egg," my mother said furiously. "And, furthermore, you may not go to Tajrish. I have eggs. What I want is a clean floor and then some bread. You can go for bread."

"Okay. I am bread," Ali said in a sorrowful voice.

The bakery was only a short distance away in a cluster of small stores. Eggs were also obtainable in the neighborhood but not always, and Ali lived in hope that he might be asked to make an emergency trip to the Tajrish bazaar, a mile down the hill from our house. Such an expedition could be stretched to an hour or more, and extra *rials* could be extracted for his return up the hill by cab. Lately, however, his luck seemed to have run out. The Missus had caught on to the ploy and no longer showed any enthusiasm for his offers to go to Tajrish.

Muttering darkly, Ali put on his shoes for the trip to the bakery, and we slithered over to the refrigerator for refreshments before the pre-dinner homework session. I, in fact, had no intention of doing any homework until I had practiced. What would normally have been a slight preference had suddenly become a crusade. I was going to make myself over from a high third horn player into a low second, and I was determined to do it in a very few days.

My room was peaceful and, like the entire house, largely innocent of furniture. Who could afford rent *and* furniture in Tehran? Well, lots of people could, but we were not among them. I sat for a moment with my horn in my lap gazing out the window at the old fig tree and at the roses along the pool, still furiously blooming in September. The sky was turning purple over the garden wall. On the other side of the house the mountains would be fading into night. "Iran," I said to myself, and a small shiver went up my spine. Then I settled in to work. Low tones, low scales, low arpeggios, all unspeakably dreary; but it was in a good cause. My natural desire for advancement in the section was now enormously reinforced by my desire to please Shaheen. It was an unbeatable combination. I struggled on and on, closing my mind to the sickly, wavering quality of the unaccustomed low notes.

After about forty-five minutes, I heard, or perhaps felt, my father's footsteps in the hall. He was the only one I knew who could actually set up a tremor in our stone floors. I put my horn down gratefully and went out to greet him. Even with my considerable height I had to stretch a bit to give him a kiss.

"Hello, hello. It's my daughter," he said. "What are you doing in there? You sound like a walrus in heat."

"Trying to transform myself into a low horn player overnight," I answered. "Poor Helmut had a horrid accident, and I moved up."

"You sound devastated. What happened to him?"

"He got hit in the mouth with a baseball."

My father, a former trombone player himself, recoiled instinctively. "My God, Jill. That's no occasion for rejoicing."

"I know," I said cheerfully. "It's ghastly, and it will probably put him out of commission for a long time. How's life in the great outer world?"

We had strolled into the living room now, and he sank into a corner of the couch which with two chairs and a coffee table formed a small island at one end. The rest of the space, as James had soon discovered, made a good skateboard track. The furniture was on loan from our landlord and was covered with lavender tufted velvet. This, combined with the shiny black plastic dining table at the other end, gave the place a style all its own.

My father considered my question. "I have a great thirst," he said finally.

"Vodka and what?"

"Vodka and anything," he said.

I went out to the kitchen where my mother and Ali were working on dinner in comparative peace and came back with a vodka and tonic.

My father stretched his huge frame on the lurid couch and sipped. "Better," he said. "The tea man at work is trying to inundate me. I no sooner finish one sickly sweet cup than

17

he's there with another, and if I show signs of turning yellow at the sight of tea, he brings me a Coke. Also sweet."

"He probably adores the ground you walk on," I said.

"Probably," my father admitted. "I do practice a sort of minimal civility."

"You're destroying the class structure," I said.

"Would it were so easy. Even the kids — my bright young Marxists — don't see the old fellow as anything but a tea machine. Of course, they were all born with silver spoons in their mouths."

"How radical are they?" I asked. "How radical do they dare to be?"

"More than you would think," he said. "They've started to trust me now and tell me all sorts of things I don't want to hear. I wish the hell they wouldn't. They know my secretary's a SAVAK agent."

"Your secretary's a what? That mousy little lady?"

"That's all right," he said. "Everybody's secretary is a SAVAK agent. The only drawback is the amount of time it takes her to read all the technical stuff I write and try to figure out if there's anything subversive in it. I could use her to more purpose for other things, but hi-ho, that's the system, my dear."

My thoughts had naturally turned to Shaheen and his reckless remarks during Farah's visit. "Don't people who mutter about the shah get run in?" I asked.

"Of course they do. And going to prison on a political charge in Iran is not something I would want to risk. Maybe some of the stories are exaggerated. But if even half the rumors about SAVAK's prisons are true, the picture is grim. I won't bore you with the details," he added after a look at my face.

"And still they talk," I said.

"More and more and louder and louder," my father answered. "Now the other side of the coin is that the secret police can't possibly lock up or even find more than a fraction of the dissidents, so the chances of getting away with a bit of random complaining are pretty good. I think the worst part must be the uncertainty — the knowledge that there are informers everywhere — the perpetual dread of the knock on the door."

"What a way to live," I said. "No wonder a lot of people want to get rid of the shah."

"At the moment it looks as if the shah is trying to mend his ways," he said. "And maybe his efforts are sincere. More likely he's trying to please the human rights people, many of whom come from that enormously useful large country across the Atlantic Ocean. I fear, however, that these good deeds are too little and too late. The shah is going to reap the whirlwind one of these days — not very soon, I think."

I gazed out the window, still thinking of Shaheen and of how he had said that his career depended upon what happened in the next year. My face must have betrayed some of my thoughts, because my father said. "Don't worry. When the revolution comes, we'll have the right kind of mark on our door."

"But only on the downstairs door," I said, referring to the fact that our landlord upstairs was a retired SAVAK colonel.

"Well, they can burn the top half of the house," my father said. He was clearly not much worried about this unattractive prospect, and neither, at the time, was I.

Ali appeared at the kitchen door. "I am dinner," he announced grandly, and we trooped across to the other end of the living room where the black table now gleamed quite cheerfully with colorful mats and beautiful Iranian glassware.

James arrived from the bedroom wing. He had an astonishing amount of paint on his hands and face which boded no good for the arithmetic problems he had certainly been assigned, but no one said anything. Dinner at our house was nearly always an amiable affair.

"I am going to get a Farsi teacher," my mother declared, as we started in on a dish of tiny Caspian Sea shrimp in a velvety curry sauce. "I know you all think it's hopeless," she continued, although nobody had so much as raised an eyebrow, "but if I have to live with Ali, and it seems as if I do, I can at least try to find out what makes him tick."

"If you find out what makes Ali tick, let us know," my father said, "but don't think that you then have the key to the country. Ali is quite exceptional."

"Well, I can at least practice on him and slow down this awful proliferation of 'I ams,'" she said. "He's driving me mad. Also it should help with the shopping. All Iran Super seems to have is canned hot dogs and frozen cardboard, and when I tried to turn myself into a lamb chop for the butcher in the bazaar, he didn't seem to understand."

"He must have been unusually obtuse," my father said. "I think your lamb chop is one of your better impersonations; but study Farsi by all means. I'll see if the company can recommend some local saint to take you on."

"Perfidious wretch!" Mum cried, and threw a small pellet of bread at him, which was swiftly returned. James showed signs of wanting to join in the fun but was quelled by a look from my father.

"Rowdiness is for grown-ups only," he said. "Life is unfair, Jamie."

"I know that," my brother said with a philosophical sigh, "but you would think it might be possible to express yourself in your own home. One expects hideous repressions at school."

"Come now," Dad said. "Surely you exaggerate."

James rolled his eyes. "The person who has recently been installed as an art teacher — notice I do not say, 'the art teacher' — is not to be believed. She must have studied art education at Auschwitz."

"I thought Community was supposed to be such a good school," my mother said. She was genuinely distressed, not having learned to take Jamie's problems with a grain of salt.

"It's a good academic school," I said, "but not much in the arts except for band, and that's just a lucky coincidence. If it weren't for the fact that an amazing conductor just happened to be looking for a job in Tehran last year, band would be as awful as art."

"Talk about unfair," James grumbled, but I wasn't about to talk much more at all. I had reminded myself of my urgent need to practice and attacked the rest of Mum's delicious dinner with unseemly haste.

Chapter 4

The next two weeks were uneventful. The evenings consisted of practicing, doing homework, and then practicing some more. We had a band concert coming up at Christmas time, and besides the mandatory old chestnuts, we were starting some really hard classical pieces transcribed for band. There were a number of very exposed duets for first and second horn and one loud, growly, horribly low second horn solo. All in all I thought I was handling it pretty well and getting better every day. For this my reward was not being criticized. I suppose I should have been grateful, but I am a person who only really thrives on encouragement, and an occasional nod of appreciation from Shaheen would have done wonders for my morale. It was said that poor Helmut had started to practice again. Insofar as one can while playing the horn, I gritted my teeth and redoubled my efforts.

The weather remained mercilessly bright, and everything in Tehran was covered with dust accumulated over five months without rain. The buildings were gray; the trees were gray; only the mountains shone as the first snow dusted the highest peaks. And gradually it grew cooler. Winter was coming at the rate of maybe one degree every other day. The shadows deepened in the garden and stayed longer. The roses still bloomed, but no one any longer felt like even a brief swim. Inevitably, I was elected for the final icy plunge to pull the plug on the swimming pool.

After all this neglect, hard work, and boredom, it was positively electrifying to see Shaheen standing by the door to my bus one day after school. That he was looking for someone was obvious; that it had to be me I could hardly doubt. My first impulse was to wonder what hideous musical crime I had committed — something perhaps so grim that it couldn't even be mentioned during rehearsal. He was straddling his horn case and looking around with fierce intensity, like a hawk that has been too long without a rabbit. When he saw me, however, his face relaxed.

"Jill, come on," he said. "I have to go to Tajrish. I'll drive you home."

While I stammered, he grabbed both our instruments and headed for the gate. I could hardly have gotten on the bus if I'd wanted to with my horn receding rapidly across the parking lot. We squeezed through the gap in the wall between two school buses and turned into the narrow street, which at this hour was choked with limousines and taxi cabs waiting for the more privileged members of the student body.

"Hey, Shaheen. This is great, but I can carry that thing," I called as I panted along behind him.

He shook his head vigorously and plowed ahead through the awful congestion. We turned the corner at the end of the compound into a quieter street and came to a stop before an emerald-green MG. I stood there speechless with admiration. It was absolutely the most appealing little car I had ever seen. Shaheen had unlocked the door and was stowing things in the space behind the two bucket seats.

"Let's see," he muttered. "Two piles of books, two French horns, one old sweater, one blanket, one pair hiking boots slightly worn, one cat carrier, two people. I think it will all go in."

I was laughing now. "I understand everything but the cat carrier. What's that for?"

He looked at me over the top of the car. "For my cat, you brilliant girl."

"I deserved that," I said, and folded myself as gracefully as possible into the right-hand seat. In the process I became suddenly aware of my long tan legs, my short white skirt, white sneakers, white tube socks. "Coltish," I thought and felt the all too familiar blush rising from somewhere around my bosom toward my face. I tucked as much as possible of my all-American lower extremities beneath the dashboard before daring to look at Shaheen again. He had started the motor and was studying the array of dials in front of him like a pilot about to take off on a hazardous mission.

"What kind of cat?" I asked.

"A Persian cat."

"I've never seen a Persian cat in Persia."

"That's not surprising," he said, "if what you mean is a long-haired creature with a flat face and no brains, because they aren't Persian at all. What I have is a true, pure-bred, unadulterated *jube* cat. I found her as a kitten wandering around our garden in the rain, and she nearly tore my hand off before I got her inside." He held out one brown hand, and I could see rows of thin, white scars.

"Charming," I said. "What's she like now?"

"A cat of milk and honey," he said.

He had now managed to get the car into the street and up to the corner, where it was halted by a tangle of limousines. This would be only the first obstacle in an hour-long drive to Shemiran. Fortunately it seemed that conversation was not going to be so difficult as I had feared.

"Shaheen," I said hesitantly, "I thought Iranians didn't like animals, I mean dogs and cats as pets."

"That's right," he said. "We don't and I don't. You Westerners are far too sentimental about animals."

"So what about this cat? I have also heard that it is practically impossible to tame *jube* cats no matter how young they are when you take them in."

"Well, it was this way," he said. "After savaging my hand and while my mother and sisters and grandmothers are all running around hysterically with bandages and hot water, this wild cat ducks under the bed. Finally peace descends, and I'm lying there enjoying the quiet but thinking unpleasant thoughts about blood poisoning, when up she jumps, sits down on the end of the bed, and starts washing herself from head to foot. This done, she begins to creep up the bed very slowly while I cower under the blankets. Then in one swift wiggle she's under the covers and curled up on my chest where she promptly falls asleep. So that's how I tamed a *jube* cat and became an animal lover in a limited way."

I had been told that Iranians were totally lacking in a sense of humor. So much for stereotypes. "What did you name her?" I asked, still fascinated by the subject.

He gave me a sidelong glance. "Kuchek Gorbe," he said.

"Oh Shaheen," I said, laughing, "you can't call her just 'Little Cat.' For one thing, she's going to grow up and be a *bozorg gorbe*, and that's an even more distressing name."

"Well, what shall I call her?" he asked. "You give her a name, and I'll try to use it."

"I couldn't possibly without seeing her," I said. "You can't just pick a cat's name out of the air."

"Really? You astonish me."

I couldn't tell whether he was teasing me or not, but I rather suspected that he was. This, I might add, was all right with me.

"It's the solemn truth," I said.

"Well then, someday you may just have to face up to all the grandmothers and visit my cat. How's your Farsi? Does it go beyond *kuchek* and *bozorg gorbe*?"

"Quite a lot beyond," I said, hoping my excitement didn't show. Had that really been an invitation? It certainly sounded like one. "I can cope pretty well in Farsi," I added, "but maybe I'm not equal to your grandmothers. How many of them are there, anyway?"

"Oh, only two most of the time, except when my father's mother is visiting. Usually it's just my mother's mother and my mother's mother's mother. Is that right?"

"It might be more concise to say 'my grandmother and my great grandmother,'" I said, "but it sounds like more old ladies the way you put it."

"That's the right impression," he said.

Having at last worked our way out of the old section of the city, we were inching through the even more horrible congestion of the commercial district with its ugly new office buildings and shops of imported goods.

"This is the worst part," I said.

He nodded. "Crowded *and* boring. Downtown when you're stopped in traffic you can look at the people. Up north you can look at the mountains. But this is nothing. Who wants to look at a bunch of clerks?"

"Mustn't be snobbish," I said.

"Why not?" he asked with genuine surprise. "You Westerners carry democracy too far."

"Why are you always talking about 'you Westerners'?" I said. "You're not so madly Oriental as far as I can see."

"You'd be surprised. You *will* be surprised," he amended. "How long have you been in Iran?"

"Three months," I said. "I know it's not long, but still . . ."

"It's not anything. You haven't got a clue." He sounded angry now, which I thought unfair.

"Well give me a chance," I said. "At least I'm trying."

Now I got the marvelous smile again. The storm seemed to have been averted. "I guess you are," he said, "and I give you credit. You're one of the very few who bother. I'm just saying that you are in a much stranger place than you may yet have realized."

I was struck, as I had been all along, by the formal elegance of Shaheen's English. Perhaps this would be a safer topic than my naive impressions of Iran.

"Where did you learn such fabulous English?" I asked.

"Had a tutor," he said, "an unfortunate English girl who lost her job in one of the schools and for some reason refused to leave Tehran. She put an ad in the *Kayhan,* and my father took her on to teach my older sisters and me. He's Oxford and Cambridge himself."

"Oxford *and* Cambridge?" I asked.

"Both," Shaheen said firmly. "Nothing but the best for the carpet king of the Tehran bazaar."

"Is that what he is?"

"Well, he's certainly one of a number of princes," Shaheen said.

I had a sudden vision of vast wealth and oriental splendor.

The thought of Persian rugs always had this effect on me. "I suppose you have lots of gorgeous rugs," I said enviously.

"Lots," he answered, "is an understatement, but so do most Iranians. Even poor people usually have a few. Carpets are our savings bank and stock market combined. They're an investment."

"If I had one, I couldn't think of selling it," I said, "any more than I would want to sell a painting I loved."

He shrugged. "Sell one beauty, get another even more spectacular. It's part of the fun, or so I am told. Unfortunately for my father, I am the only son, and I couldn't care less."

"What about your sisters?" I asked. I really knew better, but I wanted to hear what he would say.

"You've got to be joking," he said, predictably.

"No place for women in the bazaar? I think I've seen them selling pots and pans."

"Oh sure, and lots of other things. Some of them are even quite wealthy, but the real *bazaari*, particularly the rug merchants, are men. They're old-fashioned; and they're immensely powerful. My sisters, if it's any comfort to you, will probably all be professionals. One is already in medical school. They don't need the bazaar or want it, any more than I do."

"Still, they should have the right," I persisted.

"We'll worry about that when we've swept a few other problems out of the way, like your friend up there in Sa'atabad." He gave a savage jerk of his chin toward the foothills where the shah had his summer palace.

"He's not *my* friend," I protested. "Whatever made you think that? I think he's a louse."

"Your president doesn't," he said, "nor your CIA. They

28

put him there, and they're doing their best to keep him there."

"So do you think everybody in America agrees with the president or the CIA all the time? Don't be simple, Shaheen. We have just as much dissent as you do — more, probably. We just express it in different ways."

"Well, maybe," he conceded. "It seems to me that most Americans I talk to say, 'Oh, the shah's not that bad. Of course, he's a king and a dictator and he does have that nasty secret police force, but these things are probably necessary for an underdeveloped country, and look at all the great things he's done for the country,' and so on, blah, blah, blah. But his time is coming, Jill, and don't you forget it."

"That's what my father says. He knows a lot of people like you in the oil company."

"Not in the oil company surely?"

"Students. Young engineers."

"They talk to him?"

"They've started to," I said, omitting the fact that he wished they wouldn't.

"That's damned dangerous," Shaheen said.

"You're talking to me," I pointed out.

He gave me a quizzical smile. "Are you a SAVAK agent? What a poor judge of character I am."

"Well, neither is my father, obviously."

"I never thought he was. But oil company classes? My God. You might as well stand and shout your opinions up at the imperial bedroom window."

We were now squeezing through a narrow, residential street that was half blocked by some construction project, and Shaheen turned his attention to driving. This was the entrance to the Shah-an-Shahi Expressway which ran for about five miles through northern Tehran before ending in a scene of almost equal confusion near the Hilton. Since access to this beautiful little highway was so difficult, it was seldom very crowded and afforded a breathing space, if not a very substantial short cut. For some reason the city had not encroached on the expressway, so we drove between rolling dunes with the full sweep of the Alborz range spread out ahead of us. By this time we were also above the worst of the smog, and the mountains, which were often invisible from downtown, glowed softly in the late afternoon sun. To our right beyond the dunes, the low houses of East Tehran stretched into the distance, punctuated here and there by the blue domes of mosques. Far away in the northeast the solitary white cone of Damavand swam above the mist.

"I'm going to study city planning," Shaheen said suddenly. "Then after the shah is gone and we have a reasonably good government, we'll get the best consultants in the world to come here. I want to take this place apart and put it back together the way it ought to be. This ridiculous little piece of highway always makes me think of what Tehran might be like with lots of open space, clean air, good transportation, and the sight of the mountains free for everyone no matter where they live."

"That sounds like an ambitious program," I said cautiously.

He laughed. "Well, that's all I want to do — that and play first horn in a major orchestra, of course."

"Of course," I said. "Good luck, Shaheen."

"What about you?" he asked.

"Oh, I have more modest ambitions, as becomes the female of the species. I want to play the *Water Music*, preferably first horn, of course, and climb Mount Damavand."

"Stay around and we'll do the *Water Music* together," he

said. "I might even let you play first. As for Damavand, if you haven't started climbing, you'd better start now. You don't hike up there for a holiday picnic."

"I know," I said, "and I haven't even set foot on a foothill. It's discouraging."

"Where do you live?" he asked.

"Almost to Vallenjak," I said, mentioning the mountain village that marked the end of fashionable Shemiran, where we lived, and the beginning of the wild, scrubby foothills.

"No problem then. You don't even need a car. Just walk up to Vallenjak and begin."

"Do you climb?" I asked.

"Everyone in Tehran climbs," he said. "Didn't you know? I'll take you up to Darband some fine Friday, and we'll fit ourselves into the line of ill-assorted merrymakers who trek up to Pas Qaleh for tea on every holiday."

"That sounds like fun," I said, "and culturally enlightening, but not perhaps quite what I had in mind."

"Ah, but from Pas Qaleh you can go up and up. The strollers in high-heeled shoes begin to drop by the wayside after a while. The air gets thinner and the trail more difficult. You can go all the way to the Caspian Sea from the tea house at Pas Qaleh, if you don't mind carrying a pack with winter clothes, a sleeping bag, food, and so on."

The expressway had ended now, but the worst of the trip was over. We were driving north under a canopy of huge plane trees. The air was fresh and a little sharp, and here there was a definite slope to the street, although we had been climbing imperceptibly almost since we left school.

"Turn on Zaferanieh," I said, "and then take Asef, that is if you're determined to go through with this mad project."

"If you live near Vallenjak, I can hardly deposit you and your horn and your books at the foot of Zaferanieh," he said.

"That would be a swift end to a brief but beautiful friendship."

"This is true," I said, turning my head to hide a smile.

We made the turn and began to climb in earnest. "Will this be awful in winter?" I asked.

"Horrible," he said. "Sometimes people ski to work."

"Sounds like fun."

"All but the homecoming," he said, and added inexplicably, "*Barf, barf, barf.*"

"What did you say?"

"I said, 'snow, snow, snow,'" he explained, grinning.

"What a wonderful word. Wait till I tell my brother. Do you know what barf means in English?"

"I've had it explained to me," Shaheen said.

We turned off Asef onto Djalal and then down Kuche Jilá to our house.

"I hope your landlord will hire several strong *barf* shovelers," Shaheen said. "Otherwise you're going to get down in here one day and not get out for the duration."

"Well, since they have three cars to our one," I said, "maybe they've solved the problem."

As luck would have it, my mother, James, and Ali were all looking out the big front window. I don't know what the original attraction had been, but they got an eyeful when I pulled up in that green MG. Shaheen got out with me and fished all my gear from behind the seats. I felt suddenly shy, as if at the end of a long journey I were parting from someone once very close who had suddenly become a stranger.

"Don't you want to come in and have some tea and meet my weird household?" I said, looking at the ground.

"Thanks, Jill. Another time. I've got a rug to pick up, and it's getting late."

"I hope I didn't delay you," I said, feeling more inept by the second.

"Nonsense. Any time." He was back in his car, racing the motor a little.

I picked up my things and turned toward the house thinking, "another time, any time," brusque, conventional words, but still . . . I thought back over the hour we had spent together. "A brief but beautiful friendship." That was more like it.

Now how to avoid the audience at the window. Perhaps a quick dash to the bathroom with desperation written on my face. No, it was hopeless. After all, I couldn't stay in the bathroom forever. James pounced first. My brother cared next to nothing for cars, but even he could hardly be immune to the charm of Shaheen's MG.

"Jill, you sly wench," he began, "where did you find a boy friend with such a superlative car?"

"Darling, what an entrance," my mother said. "And he's fiendishly good looking. Who is he?"

"Now just one minute," I said, dropping all my stuff on the living room floor. "He's just someone I know from band. He had an errand in Tajrish, so he offered to drive me home; and lots of Iranians have MGs as you both know, so let's not make a big thing of it, okay? I'm tired and I'm hungry, and I've got a lot to do even if tomorrow is Thursday."

Unfortunately, there was yet one more party to be heard from. Ali had been frowning ferociously and struggling to express himself in a situation for which his English was clearly not going to be adequate. Good. I could pretend not to understand him. What he finally said, however, so astonished me that I was startled into answering.

"You must not go in a car with an Iranian man," Ali pro-

33

nounced, glaring at me and clenching and unclenching his hands.

"*Cherâ?*" I said. "Why? He is my friend." This simple statement, of course, contradicted much of what I had said before and added fuel to Ali's anxieties.

"Bad things will happen," he said ominously, and then went on, using words that were not in my limited vocabulary. I could guess that they involved my honor, reputation, and ultimate marriageability. This was really too much. I grabbed my horn and headed for my room. Soon my father would be home, and it cheered me to think what his reaction would be once Ali started telling him to lock up his daughter and protect her virtue.

What happened instead was that my mother told Ali to go to Tajrish, for eggs or not for all she cared, and not to come back until morning if he didn't want to. James and I were sent down the hill for bread, a chore we both enjoyed even when Ali was around. We took a piece of newspaper to protect our hands from the bread, which would be handed to us straight from the oven, and stepped out into a clear, cool night. The street lights were few and dim along Asef, and we could see the mountains looming against a crowd of stars.

It was a Wednesday night, the beginning of the weekend in Moslem countries, where Fridays are holy, and I thought happily of the two free days ahead of me. Perhaps I could make just a small, experimental foray into the foothills tomorrow.

"I'm going to start climbing in the morning," I said to James. "Want to come?"

"I'll think about it," he answered evasively. "I've got these illustrations I'm supposed to do and a model of Persepolis and . . ."

"A model of Persepolis?" I said. "That should keep you busy for a while."

"It's extra credit."

"I should hope so. Do you know how big that place is?" James nodded cheerfully and I sighed. "Never mind," I said. "It was just a passing thought."

"I'd really like to, old thing. Let me know next time you want to go."

"Okay," I said. "I'll keep you informed." In fact, I was not really disappointed. The mountains suddenly seemed very near, and a great contentment had settled over me in the starry night.

The entrance to the bakery was a dilapidated doorway with a plank stretched across it. Behind this in a small, cave-like space, were many sacks of flour, a table, and two enormous ovens. Here boys covered in equal quantities of flour and dirt worked furiously three times a day to produce the bread which is one of the staple foods of Iran. Each bakery makes only one kind of bread, and it was our good fortune to live near a source of *barbari*, that most delectable of all Middle Eastern breads. A loaf, if you could call it that, of *barbari* was nearly a yard long, golden, crisp, and buttery. It was scored before baking so that it rose in strips like a plowed field. The raised part was light as a bubble, while the furrows were pure crunch.

The chief baker glowered at us as we said our *salaams* and handed over our *toman*, the equivalent of about fourteen cents. It always saddened me a little that buying such a wonderful thing could not be a more sociable experience, but baking was an embittering profession in Iran. The shah had fixed the price of bread but not of flour, so the bakers grew poorer and angrier with each passing month of inflation. This one pocketed our coin greedily, seized a loaf from the pile which had just come from the oven, and slashed it in half with a murderous-looking knife before thrusting it into our piece of newspaper. We took turns carrying it home. A hot loaf of barbari clutched to the chest is a lovely thing in the desert night, and one has besides the chance to break off little pieces of the outer edge. Our bread always looked as if a mouse had gone busily around the entire rim before we got it home.

Chapter 5

Shaheen did not drive me home Satur-
day night after school. He was, in fact, rather remote when
I saw him during band rehearsal, and I told myself that this
was exactly what I had expected. I would worship from afar,
as I had done so often in the past. He did, however, drive
me home Sunday night and Monday and Tuesday. To justify
this addition of some forty miles to his daily commute, he
continued to maintain that he had rugs to pick up in Tajrish.

On Tuesday I said, "You know what, Shaheen? I simply
don't believe you have to pick up a rug every night after
school."

"*Cherá?*" he asked with his mocking smile, and I was immediately struck dumb.

After a bit I said, "Well, you must be exhausted, that's for
sure."

"I am," he said, "and my playing is suffering, to say nothing of Persian studies. Let's do it again tomorrow. Wear
something a little less evocative of the playing field, and
we'll stop at the Hilton for a drink."

"Terrific," I said, "but what? Never mind, I'll think of
something — I hope." My mind raced through my wardrobe,

searching for something that could be worn both to school and the Hilton. My one good pair of pants were wool, but maybe with a thin shirt I could survive the daytime temperature in South Tehran which had now dropped into the high seventies. Normally going to the Hilton would be no treat, even if I hadn't lived there when we first arrived. I couldn't help feeling that Tehran must be full of more interesting places. The Hilton, however, was every Tehrani's dream of sophisticated elegance. Anyway, it didn't matter. To be going anywhere with Shaheen — to be actually getting out of the car and going in to sit down at a table — was quite sufficient for me.

This is not to say that I didn't love every minute of our journeys in the green MG. How we talked in those early days! It was as if our lives were two wells in which each wanted to drown the other. We talked about school and music, friends and family, politics, religion, the past and the future.

The date at the Hilton was not so much a fiasco as a letdown. We sipped our drinks and made conventional conversation. Shaheen was constantly being greeted by friends who made no secret of their curiosity and disapproval. The boys stood by our table and undressed me swiftly with their insinuating dark eyes. The beautiful girls in their cocktail dresses studied my red silk shirt and black stretch pants with barely veiled contempt. I became aware that my escort was a "catch" and one whom I must somehow have landed by mistake. My own social contacts consisted in being greeted by half a dozen waiters who remembered me fondly from the summer.

When we got back in the car, Shaheen was silent for a minute, his hands resting lightly on the steering wheel. Then he took out a cigarette, lit it, and gave it to me, a

gesture of such sudden intimacy that my fingers trembled as
I accepted it. He started the motor and tossed his head as if
to clear it of the evening that lay behind us. "That's better,"
he said. "Now we can talk again."

The car was our world, and for a time it seemed as if we
would have no other. Then gradually we began to venture
forth again, not to the big hotels and nightclubs, but into the
streets, the bazaars, and the always enticing foothills. This
was what I had wanted all along, but it had taken Shaheen
a while to understand.

Chapter 6

In those early days we spoke often of the shah and of the anger and fear felt by so many who lived under his regime. Both the present plight of Iran and the stirrings of hope that were growing daily throughout the land were subjects of constant and absorbing interest to Shaheen. He talked to me more freely than ever but in a very general way. If definite plans to overthrow the government were then afoot, he was not yet aware of them. On the whole we were very carefree. Shaheen had such a joyous nature that even his anger was often cloaked in humor. But it was there, and it was deep and real. He could joke about the royal family's passion for helicopters or fume when we found a major street closed because the shah had decided to go somewhere by car. At other times there were incidents that provoked him to genuine fury.

One day we found our way blocked by a taxi that had been stopped by the police. The driver had committed some minor sin and was being questioned about it. He must have made a rude remark or, perhaps, not had the proper papers, because suddenly the policemen had dragged him out of his car and hit him on the mouth. Shaheen's fingers turned white as they tightened on the wheel. He was staring straight ahead at the scene, his whole body taut with rage. "You wait," he said in Farsi. "You wait, you sons of a burnt father. Your turn will come; and I am living for that day."

I was afraid to say anything and ashamed to be silent. "What did he do to deserve that?" I whispered finally.

Shaheen turned on me. "Nothing!" he shouted. "He did nothing but have the temerity to be alive and driving down the street in this godforsaken city. Don't you understand? You don't have to do anything to be beaten by the police when you live in a police state."

"Yes," I said. "I do understand, Shaheen." And I was suddenly aware that I had crossed some kind of threshold and that at last I did really understand. I could have said that it is always unwise to talk back to the police or that perhaps these two were unusually nasty specimens; but the stark brutality of the event had shocked me into feeling myself the anger and frustration that lay just below the surface of everyday life in Tehran.

On another day we drove out to Darrakeh, a village at the foot of one of the valleys that lead up into the mountains. Before us the range rose serenely into the blue sky. Then on our left, like some obscene growth on the lovely brown hills, I saw the walls of Evin Prison. At first I wasn't sure what it was, but a chill went through me at the sight of it, and I glanced inquiringly at Shaheen.

"That's where they'll put me one of these days when my mouth runs ahead of my common sense," he said in a disarmingly light tone of voice.

"I'll bring you a cake with a file baked inside," I said,

trying to keep the conversation from taking too serious a turn.

"You won't, you know," Shaheen said, and he wasn't joking any more. "The prisoners behind those walls — thousands of them — live without hope of cake or anything else, unless, perhaps, they hope to die. Occasionally, for reasons which are often hard to see, a few are released. Those who are more or less intact, of course, have been turned from social critics into savage enemies. Anyway, you won't get near me once I'm in there, and if you did, you wouldn't like what you saw."

I felt my stomach lurch with the shock of a real and terrible fear. "Don't!" I cried. "Don't say things like that. I can't bear it."

He looked at me pityingly. "Better to face the facts, Jill," he said. "Play time is almost over."

I was silent the rest of the way to Darrakeh — frightened and speechless. But the little village, climbing so steeply on the banks of its rushing stream, seemed to restore Shaheen's spirits. We stopped in a small shop to buy fruit for our climb up the valley, then turned to the trail with our usual enthusiasm. The soft colors of the rocks shone through the trees, and the strong sunlight poured down, bleaching the grim vision of the prison walls from my mind.

Then in mid-November a series of events occurred which, in retrospect, marked for me the actual beginning of the revolution. Certainly the two days of poetry readings at Tehran University and the violence that followed them focused the anger of the students and gave them a sense of solidarity which had been lacking before. The first news I had of the excitement came from Shaheen. It was on a Wednesday, a day when he always took me home since it was the beginning of the weekend, and I was standing in the sun at noon munching my sandwich. I saw him coming across the lawn and knew immediately that something important had happened.

"Jill, can you stand to take the bus today?" he said. "There's a thing I absolutely must go to this afternoon."

"Why not?" I said. "It wouldn't be the first time I've had to mingle with the lower orders."

"Still, it's Wednesday, and I didn't let you know. Maybe we can do something tomorrow."

"Maybe," I said. "But why all the fuss? Your guilt seems a bit much. It makes me wonder if you are off to do something I would either disapprove of or want to do myself."

He laughed. "Mind reader. I do feel that way, but really you're wrong on both counts. A very great poet, Said Sultanpour, is reading at the university. He was there yesterday too, and for some reason I didn't hear about it."

"Sounds innocent enough," I said, "and not, as you say, anything for me if it's all in Farsi."

"That's right; you'd be bored to tears," Shaheen said, clearly relieved.

"On the other hand," I said, "I can't help feeling that there's something special about this reading — something a bit more than a lovely flood of words about nightingales in perfumed gardens. Is Sultanpour a political poet by any chance?"

"Not perhaps overtly," Shaheen said, shifting from one foot to the other.

"I really think I'd like to come," I said. "You can translate the odd line here and there, and I'm up to catching a few words for myself."

"No," he said bluntly. "There's been some trouble already, and there could be more. I don't want to have to worry

43

about you if the police decide to close the reading. These things can get very rough very quickly."

I stood still, searching his face which was closed now, adamant and stern, and I felt a mixture of emotions, of which one was certainly fear and one a strong desire to be with Shaheen at what was clearly a momentous event. Finally I said, "I'm sorry. I shouldn't have asked, but I don't like to be shut out of something so important to you."

"I will describe it tomorrow," he said, "in the most vivid detail."

"All right," I said. "I guess I'll have to settle for that. Try to keep out of trouble."

"Don't worry, I will, and thanks, Jill. I'll call you tomorrow." All the gaiety and enthusiasm were back in his voice, which followed me as I trudged away toward my first afternoon class.

If Shaheen hadn't promised to call, my feeling of foreboding would not have grown to such gigantic proportions as Thursday drew to a close with still no word from him. I spent the day fidgeting, snapping at my family, trying to study or practice. And all the while the sense that something disagreeable had happened grew in my mind. I could, of course, have telephoned myself, but the more uneasy I became, the more difficult it seemed to call that unknown household for the first time, risking, perhaps, the horrible prospect of having to speak Farsi over the phone. Finally toward the end of the afternoon I went for a walk, hoping vainly that exercise and the sight of the mountains would have their usual calming effect. When I got home, my father was there, full of the news I both craved and feared.

His voice carried from the kitchen where he was fixing a drink and talking to Mum. "Those bastards," I heard him say. "Firing on a bunch of students. It's stupid too. Only strengthens the opposition . . ."

I stopped dead in the middle of the living room, feeling the color brought by the brisk November evening drain out of my face.

He came out of the kitchen. "Hello, Jill. What's the matter? You look like curds and whey."

"What demonstrations?" I said. "What have you heard? Who got shot?"

Dad gave me a startled look. "Was Shaheen at the university last night?" he asked.

"Yes!" I said violently. "I was afraid of this. What happened?"

"I don't know the details," he said, "but calm down. Hundreds of people were involved, and Shaheen is smart enough to stay out of trouble."

"That's what you think," I said. "Did they break up the reading?"

"Yes, last night they did. It seems that the poetry set off some chanting of slogans uncomplimentary to the King of Kings. The police were there just waiting for an excuse to shut things down and shove a few students around. The worst was today when there was a protest march and some shooting — not all, I fear, into the air. Some of the kids got hurt. That's all I know, but there's no reason to suppose that Shaheen was even there."

"There is every reason to suppose that Shaheen was there, and you know it, or at least you would if you knew him. He was supposed to call me today, and he didn't. Oh damn, now I really will have to telephone." For a brief moment this seemed like the worst part of the whole affair, but I sat down and dialed with determination. A cool female voice answered after a few rings. *In Jill Iskander ast,*" I began in a

45

faltering voice. *"Dust-e-Shaheen dar madrase* Community."

There was a silence as if the woman was wondering how long to let me flounder on. Then she said, "Perhaps you would prefer to speak English, mademoiselle?"

"Oh, yes," I cried. "Thank you. This is Jill Alexander. I'm a friend of Shaheen's at Community School, and I wondered — well, I had a question about a homework assignment, so could I speak to him for a minute?" I realized that I sounded about thirteen years old, but maybe that was just as well.

"I'm so sorry," said the perfect, only slightly accented voice. "Shaheen is not here just now. May I have him call you?"

"Yes, please," I said. "It's really desperately important."

"Naturally," the woman said, this time with some asperity. "I am sure that it is, and I will tell him to call. I presume he has your number?"

"Yes, thank you," I said humbly and hung up, considerably more demoralized than before. I suspected that I had just had my first encounter with Shaheen's mother, and if so, it boded no good for the future. At the moment, of course, this was the least of my worries. "He's not home," I said. "I can't find out anything. All I can do is wait."

"You care a lot for him, don't you?" my father said.

I turned on him, suddenly furious. "He's my friend! I spend half my time with him. Isn't that enough to make me a little anxious when I hear he's been shot at?"

"Quite enough, Jill. I'm sorry," he said, but I was already on the way to my room to spend what I thought at the time was the most agonizing evening of my life.

Chapter 7

Having been scared out of my wits for what seemed like an eternity, I was angry as well as relieved when I heard Shaheen's voice on the phone at nine o'clock the following morning. Not that he sounded particularly cheerful, but he certainly seemed to be unharmed.

"Where have you been? Why didn't you call?" I shouted into the receiver.

"Hey, I'm sorry, Jill. Hold on a minute. I didn't get back until late and I thought you might be asleep. Were you worried?"

"Worried?" I cried. "Why would I be worried? Asleep? Sure. I slept like a babe. Wouldn't you if you knew a friend of yours had been out getting shot at in a street riot? Come on, Shaheen."

"Well I wasn't shot," he said mildly, "but it was bad and you were right to worry. I'm really sorry. I should have called in spite of the time. Huge apologies. All right?"

"Not really," I said, "but I'm glad you're all in one piece. What happened? I only got the most awful, garbled reports." I was now feeling an absurd desire to burst into tears.

"I want to talk to you," he said, "not on the phone. Can I pick you up?"

"Come ahead. I'll try to put myself together a little in the meantime," I mumbled, and sat back limp as a rag with the phone dangling from my hand after he had hung up.

I watched from the window and ran down the path when the green MG pulled up with a spurt of dust an hour later. The whole family was home on this Friday morning, and it seemed somehow like a poor time for them to meet my friend. Shaheen must have felt the same, for he had the car in motion again almost before I had closed the door.

"Hi," I said. "You look . . ." and I stopped, at a loss for words to describe the way he looked.

He smiled in greeting, the same smile as always but his eyes had changed. They burned with a somber fire I had not seen before; and there was pain there too, and anger and, perhaps, bewilderment. "I don't know how you look," I said. "Tell me about it."

"The war has begun," he said, almost as if to himself. "There won't be any turning back from it now."

"Shaheen," I said, "I think I know what you're talking about, but would you mind telling a poor, anxious female just what has happened? Then you can generalize to your heart's content."

We were driving down Asef with the tall, white mountain peaks on our left blazing in the autumn sun. For a moment he didn't answer me as he guided the car in the steep, narrow street. A car pulled out of a parking space in front of us, and Shaheen turned into it and shut off the engine. When he faced me, I could see a graze on the cheek which had been turned away from me.

"Wednesday night when we were listening to Sultan-pour," he began in a low voice, "there was — I don't know

48

how to describe it — an incredible feeling of community. There were hundreds of us, but it was as if we had only one heart beating there in that huge, half-darkened room. He read a lot of poems — very beautiful ones, not all about liberty and the rights of man — just poems about our common humanity and about the world we live in and life and love . . ." He trailed off, and I nodded, not daring to speak. "Then," he said finally, "I don't know when it was, he spoke the word '*azadi*' — freedom — not, I suppose for the first time, but this time there came an echo from the hall, '*azadi, azadi!*' Then we were all on our feet repeating this magic word. I'll never forget it. After that it turned into more of the usual thing — chants and slogans against the shah — and it wasn't long before the lights were turned up full and the police were there shouting and bashing around with their rifles. Sultanpour got away, but the people on the platform and a few others were taken away in handcuffs. The crowd was furious, but there wasn't much we could do just then. Some of us got together afterward and decided to hold a protest march the next day. We spent the night spreading the word."

"That brings us to yesterday," I said, "and what I guess was an even more interesting event."

Shaheen looked away from me. "I don't know if I can tell you about it," he said. "At least five were killed. I didn't know them, but they were comrades — people who were marching with me. I saw one of them go down — almost at my feet."

I felt a wave of shock go through me. "That's horrible," I whispered, wanting to reach out and touch him, knowing I wouldn't reach him if I did.

He nodded, still without looking at me, but then after a moment, he straightened his shoulders and turned, and I saw that the same fire was in his eyes. "Horrible," he said. "Yes, it was. I've led too sheltered a life, and now I'll have to get used to the horrors, because this is the way it's going to be. The talking is almost over now, and action means blood. This is something you know in your head. The real experience takes a little getting used to."

I was suddenly very angry. "And we must hope it won't take long," I said in a shaking voice, "to get used to seeing people killed and, I suppose, to killing other people yourself. Soon you'll be as brutalized as they are, and then you can tear at each other's throats with a will."

"We're talking about revolution, Jill," he cried. "Did you think it was some kind of game with tin soldiers?"

"I don't know what I thought, but I do know I don't like it. And I'm frightened, Shaheen, for you and also for myself. It's all too much too fast."

"Oh look," he said, "if this is really the beginning, and it feels as if it is, you still don't need to worry. The only foreigners who had better start running are the military types who have been designing all those delightful gadgets for SA-VAK. The worst that can happen to nice, liberal people like you is that you'll have to go home and get out of the way."

"Terrific," I said. "Just when I was beginning to like the wretched place. That shows how wrong first impressions can be."

Shaheen gave me a startled look, and I could see that his mind had been far away on some imaginary battlefield. "I'm sorry," he said. "That wasn't the nicest thing to say. But history pays no heed to what individuals may want or not want. It's like a train rushing through the night, throwing all our little desires and hopes off to the side."

"And going where?" I said, still angry and hurt. "To some heroic crash more often than not."

"You don't understand," he cried. "There's nothing in your life to make you understand that it has to happen."

Hearing the anguish in his voice, I was suddenly sorry for my outburst. He was right, after all. Who was I, the lifelong resident of a country which, for all its faults, was rich and free, to judge a people who had scarcely tasted the things I took for granted? "I hope it turns out the way you want it to," I said. "Believe me, I truly do. I just have a basic distaste for bloodshed, and I don't want to go home. Selfish of me. Sorry."

"Oh God, don't apologize," Shaheen mumbled. "I don't want you to go home either. Hell no." And he fell into a gloomy silence I didn't know how to break. After a moment he reached out and switched on the engine. "Where do you want to go?" he asked. "I feel half dead. No ideas."

"Why don't you just take me home and go catch up on some sleep," I said.

"No, I don't want to do that. Sleep isn't the problem or the solution or whatever. I just want to do some normal, everyday thing with you that doesn't involve too much thought or conversation." He gave me a wan smile and turned the car out onto Asef.

At Avenue Pahlavi we turned downtown instead of going up toward the hills as we usually did. We passed the Hilton, gleaming proudly on its hilltop, and Vanak Circle with its huge statue of the old shah surrounded by the red, white, and green flags of Iran. Then we were driving along the edge of the new park which had been named, like a lot of other things, for the empress.

"You know," I said, "I've never set foot in Farah's park. Is it nice?"

"I never have either," Shaheen said. "Let's find out. I want to get out of the damn car anyway." He found an MG-

51

sized parking space in the almost solid line of cars and slid into it with practiced ease.

The park was spacious but it still had a raw, unfinished look. I thought it would be pleasant in a year or two when the grass had grown thicker and the new plantings had settled more into the landscape. But what would Tehran be like in a year or two — a free and happy city, or a bloody shambles with tank tracks over the new green? Silent again, we trudged along a winding path under ragged plane trees.

We had come up the hill from Avenue Pahlavi and now found ourselves on the edge of an artificial lake. Its surface was dotted with wild ducks who started cutting through the water in our direction the minute we appeared. "Look at the ducks," I said. "I wish we had something to feed them."

"There's a kiosk," he said. "I'll get them something." And he was off at a run toward the little refreshment stand on the other side of the pond, leaving me alone with the ducks. I watched the slender figure speeding around the end of the lake. His moods changed so swiftly, but joy was his element, the natural state to which he returned from outposts of anger and protest. He plunged into the kiosk and emerged waving something in his hand. It turned out to be a package of Tuc crackers, which were so common in Tehran that I supposed they were a special Iranian treat until I came home and found them in every supermarket.

"Too salty, do you think?" he asked as he skidded to a stop by my side.

"I doubt it. If they get a terrible thirst, there's plenty to drink," I said.

We knelt on the edge of the water and broke open the stiff cellophane packet. The ducks seemed to think as highly of Tucs as all Iranians did. They quacked and splashed and turned their neat bottoms up, chasing the golden fragments in time-honored, ducky fashion. "Look," Shaheen said, as the birds squabbled over the last crumbs, "we're giving our problems to the ducks. They don't mind, and now we feel better."

"Animals are good for people," I said. "That's a Western idea for you, but it's true."

He nodded contentedly, and we sat back on our heels watching as the ducks gradually gave up on us and started to swim in wider circles, scanning the shores for other suckers.

"You know what I want to do, only I don't know where we can do it?" Shaheen said suddenly.

"What?" I asked, somewhat apprehensively.

He laughed and I felt the inevitable blush creep into my cheeks. "Nothing really wicked," he said, "although that's another idea. We haven't played any duets yet."

I jumped to my feet, partly to hide my confusion, partly out of enthusiasm. "My parents were going out, and they should be gone by now. You've got your horn in the car, so let's go."

"To your house?" It was his turn to be dubious.

"Why not?" I asked.

"What about your brother and Ali?"

"They can put cotton in their ears," I answered cheerfully. "Come on."

"All right!" Shaheen said. "Down with politics. Up with ducks and horn players."

We ran down the hill, laughing under the autumn trees that no longer seemed gray and tattered, and piled into the car. Shaheen made a U-turn on Avenue Pahlavi, which showed how eager he must be to get on with our project, and we headed north again.

Chapter 8

The house seemed very empty when we stepped through the front door. James might well be holed up in his room, but Ali had almost certainly gone out, and I thought that for a day which had begun so badly, this one was definitely taking a turn for the better. Shaheen put down his horn and surveyed the living room — the lavender furniture, the black table, the huge vacant spaces in between — with an expression of disbelief. "Minimalist," he said after a moment. "Is that what you call it?"

"Except for the couch and chairs," I said. "They belong to a less austere tradition."

"What you need is obvious," he said. "One hell of a big carpet would solve all of your problems."

"So would two thousand dollars used in a number of ways," I said.

"Oh, don't worry about that," Shaheen said, striding across the room and throwing his jacket on one of the chairs. "I'll lend you one."

"You can't do that!"

"Why not? You can have one almost forever on approval. If you get rich suddenly, you can buy it at a fraction of what it would cost in America. If not, we simply take it back."

"But Shaheen," I protested, "we can't walk around on a beautiful and hideously expensive rug for months and months and then just say, "Sorry. It was a nice thing to have around, but no thanks after all.'"

"Nonsense," he said. "Being walked on is good for Persian rugs. Breaks them in. You know sometimes the merchants put them out in the street and let cars drive over them." I shuddered, but he went on firmly. I had never seen him in a rug merchant mode before, and it had a certain fascination. "There's a big red and gold Turkoman in the shop right now," he said, "which would be really smashing in here. Warmth and richness. That's what this place needs."

"Red and gold?" I said, eyeing the furniture.

Shaheen followed my glance. "You'll have to do something about that stuff, of course," he said.

"Shaheen, we can't. We have no money, strange as that may seem to you, and besides, we don't want to reupholster the Fahouris' ghastly chairs."

He shrugged. "Oh well then," he said. "There's a rug for every situation hiding somewhere in the bazaar, even one that will do something for those chairs. After all, they're Iranian chairs, much as I hate to admit it, so there must be an Iranian rug to go with them. I'll keep my eyes open. And now to more important matters. Get your horn, girl. We don't want to stand around all day nattering about rugs."

"Do you want to play out here or in my room?" I asked. "My room is a bit less cathedral-like but still very live."

"Out here, by all means. I can hardly wait," he said, bending over his horn case.

55

By the time I had come back with my instrument and stand, Shaheen had dragged two dining chairs to the center of the living room and was starting to run through scales and arpeggios with even more than his usual uninhibited virtuosity. I sat down and joined in with my own more modest warm-up routine. The sound of two horns doing different things in that room was horrendous, and after a moment I saw James creep around the corner from the bedroom wing. He looked like some small animal that has popped out of its hole at the sound of the hunt. I nodded to him as I took a breath, and after a brief, wide-eyed stare, he disappeared again. This was the only interruption we had during the next glorious hour, although the phone may well have rung itself off the hook without our knowing it.

After we had warmed up, Shaheen bent over and rummaged through the stack of music by his side. He straightened up, waving Handel's *Water Music* triumphantly in my face. "You've got it!" I cried. "Fantastic. I didn't even know you owned it."

"And the First Brandenburg Concerto, but we'll save that until we're really warmed up. Do you want to play first?"

"Help," I said. "Don't threaten me with the Brandenburg. I'll lose my nerve, and no, I don't want to play first. If I am to survive this orgy at all, I'll have to conserve my strength."

"It's not very low, anyway," he said, "nor very high either. Just a nice cozy middle register. You'll love it. Watch the intonation, though. If this doesn't ring like a bell, it's no good at all."

I nodded humbly, and we launched into the *Water Music*. Except for some of the trills, it was not too difficult for me, nor did I have any trouble staying in tune. Shaheen was an aggressive player, but so, on my better days, was I, and this was surely the best day I had ever had. The beautiful, clear chords rang out as shafts of late afternoon sun poured through the windows; the air was radiant with sound and light. We were carried away by our sonority and by the headlong pace of the music, and when the last notes had died away, we sat back and gave a double sigh of contentment.

"Now for the Brandenburg," Shaheen said after a moment.

"Let's not," I said. "I'll foul it up for sure, and I don't want to spoil this wonderful feeling."

"Come on. It will be fun. You'll see." He was already digging through his music.

Playing the Brandenburg, or portions of it, really was fun, if also rather silly. Shaheen missed almost as many notes as I did, which was not surprising since his part was fiendishly high, and even he must have been tiring slightly. We took it at a breakneck speed, and ended up in a tangle about halfway through the allegro spluttering and laughing wildly.

It was at this point that Ali made his entrance. He came charging through the front door and stood glaring at us from across the room. "Missus Jill," he said at last, "I am music no," and stamped off toward the kitchen. This threw us into another explosion of mirth.

Finally Shaheen said, "I suppose that was the famous Ali." I nodded speechlessly. "And what the hell was he trying to say?"

"We never know," I said, choking down the last of my giggles, "unless he speaks Farsi, which he does only in moments of absolute desperation. This is one of the things that makes living with him such a treat. I would guess, from my long experience as an interpreter, that he is expressing disapproval of both French horn music and you, or at least of your unchaperoned presence in our house."

"I'll have to take that lad in hand some day," Shaheen said.

"Oh, please do," I said. "That would be ever so diverting."

Shaheen laughed and stood up. "I must go now," he said. "It's been an exhausting day, what with one emotion and another. We'll play again soon, perhaps after school at my house. There's really no reason why we can't. My family — even my grandmothers — are far more progressive than your houseboy, and some of them actually like our kind of music."

"Marvelous," I said. "Any time. But I suppose your house is totally muffled in rugs."

"In fact, it has considerably better acoustics than this barn," he said, "but I wouldn't have missed those echoes for anything."

I watched contentedly as he put away his horn and retrieved his jacket. Incredible that only a few hours ago we had been sitting in the car, angry and afraid, shaken by the imminence of war and separation. If only he's wrong, I thought, and we still have a little time. And at that moment it seemed that catastrophe might be postponed indefinitely — that we could go on and on in this cocoon of happiness, troubled only by the unfolding complexities of our relationship.

Chapter 9

In the weeks that followed the poetry readings it seemed as though my wish for an interlude of peace had been granted. The government closed the university, and the students snarled quietly with impotent rage. They also spent their free time to good effect, meeting and plotting to perfect their revolutionary organization. Nothing occurred, however, that even approached the violence of the protest march, and the population of Tehran, both foreign and Iranian, went about its business with only the usual quota of grumbling and discontent.

While all of this was going on, my daily life stayed much the same. I did my homework, practiced my horn, lived out the usual ambivalent scenes of family life. On Thanksgiving we had American friends to dinner — the Enrights, a thoroughly nice, impossibly boring couple whose company we endured because their daughter was my closest friend.

Barbara and I had books in common. We were largely incompatible in other ways, but a love of books — some of them the same books — is a substantial bond. She was an unsettling mixture of poet-dreamer and social butterfly, so our rapport faded in and out depending on her mood of the moment. This slightly shaky friendship came under severe strain when I started spending half my time with Shaheen. In the first place, although Barbara had several dazzling senior boys on the phone every night of her life, there was undoubtedly an element of jealousy. Her young men might be more eligible, but mine was more mysterious. She wanted me to "tell all," and normally I would have been delighted. Now something held me back. I told next to nothing, and it drove her wild.

Anyway, that the Enrights should have Thanksgiving at our house or we at theirs was inevitable, since they were the only family we knew well in Tehran, although it was puzzling that my mother had been elected to cook. My father once said that my mother would not know a turkey if it walked up and bit her. This is slanderous and untrue. She would not only know a turkey, she would instantly think of countless exotic and wonderful ways of dealing with it in the kitchen. None of these, however, would involve filling it up with chunks of dry bread and sticking it in the oven for the afternoon.

To make matters worse, it seemed that we might be deprived of the services of Ali on this festive but exhausting occasion. He emerged from his room that morning later than usual and, without even pausing in the kitchen, wove his way unsteadily to the living room where he sank with a groan into one of the lavender chairs. Mum looked up from her borrowed copy of *The Joy of Cooking* to watch his uneven progress. "If I didn't know better," she said, "I would think that boy had been drinking."

"What makes you think you know better?" I asked.

"He's a devout Moslem," my mother said, indignantly.

I went to the living room and stood in front of Ali who had

his head in his hands. "Oh, Missus Jill," he moaned. "I am vodka no."

"I think you were vodka yes," I said, "but what happened? In Farsi, please. It will be faster."

There wasn't much of a story. He had met two friends in Tajrish. They had spent some time hopelessly eyeing the chador-wrapped young ladies of the district until, weakened by despair, one of them had gone to the Armenian liquor store for a bottle of vodka. This they had consumed straight in the privacy of one of Shemiran's numerous vacant lots. They were not, needless to say, very experienced drinkers, and the results were predictable — unrestrained joy followed by unrelieved gloom, both sensations greatly heightened by the sense of sin. "Allah will punish me," Ali declared, making an unconvincing attempt to tear his hair.

I searched my mind for the tenses of Farsi. "Allah *has* punished you," I said triumphantly, "and what about our festival dinner?"

Mum had now come out of the kitchen and was looking down at Ali with a frown. To be fair, he was really quite fond of her, if not of me. "Oh, Missus, I will try," he said. "I abase myself at your feet."

"He abases himself at your feet," I translated.

"Oh, stop it," she cried. "That's awful. Never mind, Ali. Go to bed. *Khab, khab,* Ali," she added, making shooing motions toward his room.

Our servantless Thanksgiving dinner turned out, with a bit of guidance from *The Joy*, to be quite easy for a cook as experienced as my mother, and the end result was more than edible. Cleaning up was a different matter. After dinner Mum and I surveyed the kitchen and concluded that the only solution was to set fire to it and start over in a new house. Marjorie Enright, on the other hand, was in her element. Nothing was cheerier, she said, than to go out into the kitchen and have a good chat over the dishpan. Maybe so, maybe not, but she was definitely the right person in the right place. Without her, we would probably be wallowing in turkey grease to this day.

The servant crisis shortened my time alone with Barbara, and for this I was both glad and sorry. I had been missing our earlier intimacy — the letting down of hair, the peaceful reads lying on the floor of her room or mine surrounded by books until far into the night. After the kitchen was cleaned up, we left the adults trying to keep awake over their brandy and went back to my room. My horn lay out on the single straight chair, gleaming softly in the lamplight. I seldom put it in its case except to go to rehearsal. If it sat there in the middle of the room, I was more likely to sit down and play for a while without making a big deal of it. Barbara gave the horn a wide berth on her way to the book shelves.

"I'm always afraid I'm going to knock your baby on the floor," she said.

"Such clumsiness could only be intentional," I said. "It's really very heavy and not likely to fall without a push."

"Practicing a lot?" Barbara asked, turning toward the books. Her casual tone didn't fool me one bit. Everybody thought I practiced for the sole purpose of pleasing Shaheen, and, like all great slanders, there was enough truth in the allegation to make me furious. I had been passionately fond of the horn before I even came to Iran, so the fact that a personal factor made me work a little harder was merely a bonus. At least so it seemed to me.

"Not so much," I said. "I'm just too lazy to put it away."

"Sure, Jill, sure," Barbara said. She abandoned the shelves and went over to flop on my bed. For once my books had failed to fascinate her. I wondered if she was losing her mental grip. This could happen even to an intellectual teenager under certain very severe conditions usually involving sex. "You don't care what the first horn player thinks about your playing. That's good," she continued.

"One always cares what the section head thinks," I said severely, "providing that the opinion of the section head is worth considering, which certainly isn't always the case."

"You're being a prig," she said.

I sighed and went over to my tape recorder, put a Simon and Garfunkel on, and sank down on the floor next to the bed. "Come on, Barbara," I said. "Don't be difficult. Tell me about your love life."

"I'd rather hear about yours," she said stubbornly. "Mine hasn't changed all that much since the last time I told you all about it and you gazed off into space with your mind a million miles away."

"Listen," I said, "and listen well. I haven't got a love life. I have a very good friend of the male gender who is madly interested in a lot of the same things I am madly interested in. He also owns a very nice car and drives me home a lot. This I enjoy, and it is not my fault that half of Community School has nothing better to do but speculate on what goes on between here and South Tehran. You're all jealous because I don't have to take the school bus. That's what it is."

"You mean all you do is ride around in the car and talk?" Barbara asked.

"We've done a little climbing," I admitted, "and prowling through the bazaar — that sort of thing."

"Well, just watch your step," she said. "That one's got a reputation, in case you didn't know."

I laughed. "First you try to pry the secrets of a torrid romance out of me, and then you warn me to protect my virtue,"

I said. "Make up your mind." At the same time that word, "reputation," was going round and round in my head. Reputation, reputation, what kind of reputation? I was damned if I was going to ask, and for this strength of character I still give myself high marks.

"Oh, you're hopeless. I give up." Barbara sat up, as if to signify that the cozy-chat part of the evening was over.

"Just as well," I said. "Now look at what I found at the Kayvan, practically brand new." I flourished a copy of Roloff Beny's beautiful book of photographs, *Persia, Bridge of Turquoise*. Finding this expensive book secondhand had been a real triumph. Barbara leapt upon it with cries of delight. Her enthusiasm for daily life in Tehran was slight, but these ravishing pictures of mosques and ruins and mountain tribesmen were fuel to her romantic imagination. We pored over the book for an hour, pointing out favorite scenes and trying, with little success, to decipher the scraps of Persian poetry. When her mother knocked on the door to say that it was time to go, we parted with more affection than we had felt for some weeks.

"Let's make a foray to the Kayvan soon," Barbara said as we were all standing at the door. "I'm wallowing in babysitting money."

"Lucky you," my father said. "Jill has given up wealth for love."

"Et tu, Brute," I said. I was keeping it light, but I really did feel betrayed. He was one person who should have known better. Probably it was all that disgusting brandy taking its toll.

"Don't be cross, angel," my mother said as she closed the door on our guests. "It was a lovely Thanksgiving, and I'm always so thankful to put another one behind us."

"And we didn't have to hear Ali moaning and singing mournful Persian songs over the dishes," I added.

"Well, as to that," she said, "I could have stood to put my feet up after dessert, but it turned out all right. Why are some women given such an overdose of efficiency, and others get hardly any at all?"

"Just stay the way you are," my father said, putting his arm around her. "I wouldn't trade you for ten Marjories."

"Now there would be a domestic whirlwind," I said. "Well, goodnight all."

They said good night, still holding on to each other, and I slipped back to my room thinking, as I so often did, that having parents who loved each other after years and years must be the luckiest part of my life.

Chapter 10

The Sunday after Thanksgiving Helmut came back to the horn section, as big and complacent and Teutonically competent as ever. Naturally, after a brief tryout, he was given his place back, and I moved gracefully down to third horn. The entire band watched this maneuver with an avid interest which I felt was far out of proportion to its entertainment value. People changed chairs all the time, up and down and up and down. What was so fascinating about this one? As if I didn't know. Actually the public aspect of my demotion was the only thing I really minded. I sat next to Shaheen in a far more intimate place almost every day, and I had never really liked low horn.

Shaheen found me later during a class break sitting in the sun in a warm corner where one of the old buildings joined another. He stood there frowning down at me as if at a loss for words, and I didn't give him any help. "Well, I can't take you home today either," is what he finally said. "We've got relatives from Isfahan. I have to go straight home."

I felt gratified and relaxed. "Shaheen," I said, "what are you so guilty about?"

"You don't mind?" he asked.

"About what?"

"About that lump taking your place, of course."

"Actually not," I said, relenting. "I really like third better because it's high, and you know what the usual line of succession to first horn is."

He nodded. "Third, second, fourth. But since we graduate at the same time, I don't see what consolation that is."

"Arrogant brute," I said affectionately. "Sit down and don't hover."

He crouched in the sun beside me. "I know," he said. "You like to be a soloist. The high horns are the ones that get heard."

"You should know," I said.

He smiled and went on. "Cutting through the rest of the ensemble, a cry of defiance out of the storm — that sort of thing."

"Exactly that sort of thing," I said.

We understood each other. Shaheen was making fun of both of us with his purple prose, but there was a grain of truth in his words. I think even the most hard-nosed professional hack would secretly agree that there is a mystique to French horn playing. There is that moment for which one waits with quickened pulse when the horn call rises clear out of a well of silence or breaks above the rush of orchestral sound. Then one is Roland in the forest of Roncesvalles rallying his small band in a hopeless cause. It is an ancient call of knights and kings, and its power is amplified for the player by the sheer terror which so often accompanies its performance.

"I wonder if Helmut feels this way," Shaheen said.

"He should," I said doubtfully, "what with Wagner and all, but somehow it doesn't seem possible."

Shaheen laughed and jumped up. "Do you know," he

said, "you have brightened my life remarkably in the last two months." And with that he turned away sharply and disappeared around an angle of the building, leaving me to reverberate there in my corner like a plucked string.

More about music. The MG, of course, was equipped with a marvelous radio, and there was an hour of classical Western music on one of the Iranian stations at four o'clock. This soothed our nerves as we battled northward through the traffic after school and provided extra fuel for conversation.

At other times of day the radio was more of a problem. Out of deference to my nationality in the early days of our friendship Shaheen kept it tuned to the American armed forces station. Thinking he must like this tripe, I endured in silence. It wasn't that I disliked popular music. I liked rock to dance to and folkier things for daydreaming and doing homework, but the music they played on that station was the bottom of the barrel. As an alternative there were the talk shows. We had only listened to a few of these when I went into open rebellion. It was a program called "How I Met My First Love" and featured interviews with army housewives.

"Shaheen, help!" I said after about ten minutes of this. "Isn't there anything else on — anything at all?"

He turned the radio down. "Not your sort of thing? I thought it would be a little reminder of home."

"You did not," I said. "And even the worst daytime radio at home is better than that. Let's just have silence if there isn't any decent music."

"Only Persian music at this time of day."

"What's wrong with Persian music?" I asked.

"It's strange."

"So what? I've got an open mind. Maybe I'll come to like it. In fact, I've already heard some I liked."

"Iranian-American pop," he said scornfully. "Successfully combining the worst features of both countries."

"I thought what I heard was very pretty," I said, "but then, I'm not as critical as you are."

"Not such a snob, you mean."

"You said it, I didn't."

Shaheen stretched behind the steering wheel. We were near the expressway now and firmly stuck in traffic.

"So what about old Persian music before Western corruption set in?" I asked.

A faraway look came into his eye. "That's another story," he said. "You'll find it difficult, but let's see what I can find. There's usually some on the radio for the old people."

At this point the traffic loosened up, and we shot forward a whole half block into the bottleneck at the Shah-an-Shahi. There was a babble of Farsi from the radio. "This should do it," Shaheen said, after listening for a moment. "In fact, excellent. Solo *tar* and *dombec*. No singing, which is what Westerners find hardest to take." He leaned back, prepared to lecture over the voice of the announcer. "The tar is what you might expect from the name, but older, smaller, rounded, not wide and flat like the guitar. They've been playing it for centuries, always in small groups or alone, because often music had to be hidden away in people's homes. The mullahs have never been fond of music."

The snarl of traffic suddenly resolved itself, and we slid out onto the expressway. "The dombec is a hand drum," Shaheen went on, "but wait. You'll see."

The announcer had stopped talking, and into the silence came a quick patter of notes from the tar. At first it seemed

69

to wander, the small, intricate statements punctuated by moments of expectant stillness. The notes were soft, tentative, but an almost palpable tension was growing. Suddenly the dombec entered with a fierce, heavy beat sustained by finger strokes of incredible speed and complexity. Now both instruments were building towards a climax — building, breaking off, building again. As it went on and on, I found I was holding my breath and my heart was racing. I stared out at the desolate beauty of the mountains and felt the music carry me back through centuries of solitude and desire. I sensed the elaborate constructs of an ancient civilization and felt the cruel passion of the desert. The music grew to an almost unbearable intensity and then, suddenly, it stopped. I heard Shaheen sigh sharply as if he, too, had been holding his breath. "*Aré!*" he said softly. "Yes. That's it."

He turned down the radio and glanced over to see my reaction. "I didn't think you'd get it so fast," he said.

"I must have been ready for it. My God, Shaheen, where has this music been all my life?"

"Right here on Radio Tehran," he said, "but most people don't care for it any more. They want easy listening, and this has to be total immersion. I'll take you to a concert sometime. This old music is hard to find but well worth the search. It's good to be able to see the players — to watch their fingers and their faces. Another good thing is to close your eyes and listen in the dark."

"I'd be afraid," I said.

"Afraid?"

"Afraid of having my mind stolen away — afraid of going too far into the music and not being able to get back." I laughed a little shakily. "That sounds crazy, I know, but can you guess what I mean?"

He looked at me for a moment before answering. Then

he said, "I find that I am always underestimating you. Why is that, do you suppose?"

"You listen to too many army wives telling how they met their first loves," I explained. "It's a wonder you ever so much as looked at an American girl."

Shaheen grinned. "The looking was no problem," he said. "Talking to one took more determination."

He turned the radio up again, and we listened to more music as the car slipped through the brown dunes. I remembered that I had heard these sounds before, unregarded fragments that now made sense. The classical music of Iran might not be popular, but it was part of the fabric of life even in sophisticated Tehran. Soon it would be part of my life — its rhythms in my blood, its strange, compelling patterns imprinted in my mind. I would hear them in some far city of the West and feel again this surge of passion, of loneliness, and of joy.

Chapter 11

We went at last on the promised climb to Pas Qaleh. It was now early December, and the high passes were filled with snow. There were even patches of white here and there in the little parking lot where the road ends at the top of the village of Darband, but the sun was warm on our backs as we climbed the long flight of stairs past the silent machinery of the ski lift. As far as I know, the lift operates only in the summer when it gives hikers a short boost up to the first tea house. I cast a wistful glance up at the empty cars swinging above my head. The ride looked as if it would be fun and a bit scary. Perhaps in one of those cars I could shriek and clutch at Shaheen and he would put his arm around me. On the other hand, I couldn't imagine myself doing any such thing.

After the first steep ascent, the trail became wider and the climb more gradual as it followed the top of the ridge high above the valley that ends at Pas Qaleh. Where the trail was wide enough we walked abreast, and an almost palpable current flowed between us. I thought I could feel our hands reaching out across that tiny gap, and though the gap remained, the air around us shimmered with an intense, silently communicated happiness.

Once past the top of the ski lift, we could see the village at the head of the valley, its brown houses rising above terraces of bare fruit trees. "It must be beautiful in spring," I said, thinking of how the trees would blossom against the somber walls and the gray rock.

Shaheen nodded. "We'll come back," he said, "but so will a lot of other people. The off season has its compensations."

It was also an off day — a weekday when, for some reason, we had no school. We had the trail to ourselves, and it was hard to believe that on a bright, spring Friday it would hold a solid line of people toiling upward in the sun.

At the top of the valley the trail turned right and crossed a wooden bridge over a waterfall. There on the other side was the tea house of Pas Qaleh, with the river running right through the middle of it. The structure seemed to be attached to the mountainside and was built entirely out of flattened tin cans. The front was open to the trail, to the river, and to the view down the valley. It was still very warm in spite of the altitude, and we stopped to look out over Darband and Tajrish, out over all of Tehran as far as the tiny pencil strokes of the refinery chimneys at Shahr-e-Rey.

In front of the tea house was a table piled with things to eat — pomegranates glowing like rubies in the sun, oranges, ripe tomatoes, a folded pile of brown lavash, white eggs — the makings of a feast. Shaheen asked if I were hungry. He was speaking Farsi, as he sometimes did with me. I never knew what set him off, but perhaps on occasions such as this he felt close to the spirit of his country and wanted to express himself, even to me, in its language. His Farsi was very clear and beautiful, and I seldom had trouble understanding him.

73

Certainly this question was no problem. Yes, I was hungry — ravenous, in fact, and also ready to sit down in this entrancing place.

There were no tables or chairs in the dim interior. Instead it was furnished with long benches covered with slightly mangy carpet. On these one sat and ate and even, Shaheen said, might take a nap in warmer weather. I thought how pleasant it would be to lie there in the dappled light with the mountain landscape sparkling outside and the voice of the stream running past my head. We were alone in the tea house except for the two peasant women who were its proprietors. They were brown and cheerful-looking and wore their chadors very casually like tribal people with a good deal of their hair and all of their faces showing. One who was washing dishes in the stream even had her ragged draperies tucked up to her knees. We sat on the bench nearest the view, and the other woman brought us tea. Shaheen followed her back to the table at the door where the two of them in spirited conference selected the ingredients of an omelet. He was curiously gentle with these mountain women and without the touch of arrogance I had noticed when he spoke with working people in the city.

The omelet came on a single tray with a large spoon for each of us and a pile of lavash in the center. Lavash is that round, floppy bread much like a huge pancake which is used so often in the Middle East to wrap around other food. Only the best lavash has much taste, but this seemed very good, especially considering that it had probably come up from Tehran on the back of a donkey. Actually I was in no condition to judge. In that state of bliss I might well have eaten a piece of old inner tube and pronounced it food for the gods. Our omelet, however, would have pleased the most

74

jaded gourmet. The tray reposed between us on the bench at thigh level, and I watched Shaheen for a clue as to the most efficient method of consumption. To my astonishment, he put the omelet in the lavash, rolled it up, and ate it all with his right hand. I knew, of course, that these were proper Moslem table manners but had never seen him do it before. He was amazingly deft about the whole thing. I shook my head and proceeded by trial and error with both hands.

The woman brought more tea and, surprisingly, glasses of water. She spoke for the first time since greeting us at the door. "This is the water of the mountain," she said. "It is the best water in the world." It was. We sipped and smiled at her and at each other. Silently we reached to the center of the tray and shared the lavash. I remembered reading that bread was sacred, and now it seemed to be true. We had known each other well, even eaten together, but this was different. This was communion.

Outside after lunch the sun dazzled our eyes as we gazed around the village and the mountain sides. "Up or down?" Shaheen asked. I looked for the trail. There it was, going straight up out of the roof of the tea house — all the way to Chalus on the Caspian Sea. One part of me wanted to climb on and on, but another part had had enough. "Let's go down," I said. "I feel somehow . . ." I groped for the right word in Farsi and found instead the Iranians' favorite English word. "Finished," I concluded. "Finished *hastam*. But it's been a perfect day. When can we come back?"

He looked up at the white slopes that came almost to our feet. "In another week you won't be able to find this place in the snow," he said. "Although life does go on up here in the winter, God knows how. As soon as it melts we'll be back — in March I promise you, if not before."

I gave the tea house one last, fond glance and turned back over the bridge, thinking how good it was to talk of an event that lay so far ahead, feeling my happiness spin out across the unknown months like a rainbow.

Chapter 12

As the year drew to a close, the luxurious houses scattered over the hills of Shemiran began to sparkle with Christmas trees. Not only the homes of foreigners and of Iranian Christians shone with red and green and the silver of tinsel, but also those of rich, westernized Moslems, in a cheerful, eclectic display that was not to be seen again in Iran. Meanwhile, in the narrow streets of South Tehran, the grim drama of Moharram was being played out. Moharram is the terrible month of mourning for Hossein, murdered by the caliph's soldiers at Kerbala in the seventh century. It is the parable of an oppressed and martyred people, a natural theater for anger and revolt. So while the birth of Christ was celebrated in the foothills, the black processions marched in the south, crying the name of Hossein with anguish and with a new-found rage. It was a curious feature of that strange and dislocated time that neither group of celebrants paid much attention to the other. That the Christmas lights were the last, brave flicker of a dying way of life and that the future of Iran was unfolding under the dark banners of Moharram was a fact of which we were mercifully unaware.

Certainly our family was very merry in its new home, in

its new country. We had always spent a lot of creative energy on Christmas, and this one called for a special effort. While Dad plotted to winkle a suckling pig out of the Armenian community, Mum brooded over unconventional ways to cook it. (We would be alone for this holiday dinner, and if we wanted to consume Indonesian roast pig by the light of the Christmas tree, there would be no one to raise an eyebrow.)

James and I devoted ourselves to the production of Christmas tree ornaments. He bought some clay and began an assembly line of fanciful little animals, gnomes, long-bearded dwarfs, and mock-ferocious trolls. I wandered the bazaar, looking at everything from a new point of view, trying to see small, commonplace objects as potential decorations. Pine cones and cranberries were not to be found in Tehran, but soon I began to see other exciting possibilities. Poppy seeds, cardamom, and star anise were sold in their own intricate little pods, which could be gilded. Persian gumdrops came in wonderful, jewel-like colors, but were almost too good to be allowed to dry out on the tree. In a pottery shop downtown I found ceramic stars glazed in the brilliant lapis blue of donkey beads.

On December 23, as if to confirm us in the delusion that everything was being laid on for our happiness, about a foot of snow fell on our neighborhood. I say "on our neighborhood," because a mile away down the hill there was hardly any. Fortunately we had been forehanded with our shopping, and it wasn't until the day after Christmas that my father had to face the grim realities of which we had been warned. For bread and other small necessities we walked to the little stores of Asef, knee deep in barf, to quote my brother's delighted description.

A heavy snowfall in the hills above Tehran is strange to

one accustomed to the blustering gales of New England. There is seldom any wind. The woolly clouds gather in late afternoon, and all night long the snow comes down softly as if from a huge flour-sifter somewhere in the dark, enormous sky. Morning reveals a world transformed. Not only the mountains, but the garden, the swimming pool, the fig tree, the flat-roofed houses are blanketed in white.

These flat roofs present a problem. For a brief season every year you have desert architecture in an alpine climate. The snow that falls in the hills would be a burden to the strongest house, and strength is not a prime feature of the Shemiran villa. Leaks and even cave-ins are common, so immediately after a big snowfall, wizened and lightly dressed servants can be seen on all the rooftops pushing the stuff off into the street with brooms. This further complicates the life of the hapless driver.

For the moment, however, we were pleased to stay at home. Free of any obligations except to ourselves, we strung our lights and hung our curious ornaments on the handsome tree we had brought up from Pahlavi just before the storm. We had music and wine and piles of elaborately wrapped presents which we had bought for each other with our usual carefree disregard of the financial future.

Only the gloomy presence of Ali marred the festive atmosphere. He was in mourning for Hossein but seemed uninterested in going out to march with his fellow mourners. Perhaps the prospect of keeping our kitchen clean was preferable to that of walking through the rain of South Tehran and beating himself with chains. Still, the lovely roast piggy smells that drifted from our oven on Christmas day must have driven him nearly wild — one way or another — as he ate his bowl of leftover chicken and rice. My parents gave him a stylish Italian sweater, which was a mild success, at least compared to my gift of an alarm clock. Most of the time he spent in his room gazing, I suppose, with mournful intensity at his walls, which were covered floor to ceiling with pinups of American movie stars. We tried to put him out of our minds as we threw ourselves into our traditional celebrations.

All in all, out of many years of spectacular family Christmases, the one in Tehran stands out in my mind. There was something very special about it — very private, very much our own, closed in as we were by snow and an alien culture. And, although many intensely happy days were still to come, it was the last time we were completely free of worry and doubt.

Chapter 13

Two days after Christmas it snowed again, and Shemiran became a network of ski slopes. James and I decided to sled down to the Enrights' house, which was near the Hilton in Mahmudiyeh. I had a mild desire for a cozy gossip with Barbara, and James would probably tramp over to the hotel to browse longingly through the Asterix books at the newsstand and order a Coke in the bar. The sledding was wonderful if hazardous, since there were still some cars, especially on Asef, and their drivers were understandably indifferent to our safety. About halfway down, however, we were able to turn off to the right onto a series of smaller streets which carried little traffic in the best of weather. There were Iranian children sledding too. The boys wore an assortment of conventional winter clothes, but we saw two little girls in chadors. The voluminous black cloth billowed around them as they slid, revealing glimpses of jeans and Norwegian ski sweaters underneath. "Look out for them," James shouted in my ear. "One of those things gets caught under the runners and they'll be all over the road." His fears were unfounded, however, and they sped on ahead of us like a pair of crows against the snow, laughing and shrieking all the way.

The road was beginning to show bare patches by the time we reached our destination, and the Enrights' driveway was clear. Life in the winter must have been simpler at their altitude but also a lot less fun. I didn't envy them one bit and doubted if my father did, except, perhaps, when he was kneeling in the slush to switch the chains on the car.

Marjorie had cocoa and cookies ready for us. The cookies were Oreos, which had been acquired by devious and elaborate means from the American PX. This is not to say that both of these homey treats weren't extremely welcome after our snowy trip. (My cynicism has its limits and falls far short of condemning Oreos and hot chocolate after sledding.) James consumed his and took off for the hotel, while Barbara and I carried second helpings back to her room.

My friend sank to the floor in one fluid movement, ending up cross-legged next to a very impressive and obviously new tape recorder. "Hey, look at that," I said, going down on my knees beside this beautiful object. "Santa must have loved you this year."

"You could say that," Barbara answered, "but you know, it was the only thing I got. When everybody gets only one thing, it makes for a short Christmas morning."

Barbara had paid a brief visit to our house just before the first snow and had seen the piles of presents around the tree like some charity set-up for a mob of underprivileged children. "Well, mine were mostly pretty small," I said, "and, besides, my father's crazy. Which would you rather have, a crazy father or a gorgeous new tape recorder?"

"That's easy," she said, "a crazy father. I had a perfectly good machine before — well, not as good as this one, but good enough."

"Speaking of which, what did you do with it?" I asked, thinking of my own box, which was on its last legs and never had amounted to much. It was the kind you buy to study language tapes, and only the desperate would think of actually playing music on it.

"Sold it," Barbara said briefly. She was looking rather guilty, as well she might.

"Already?" I said. "You might at least have asked me."

"I should have," she said. "I suppose you had some Christmas money."

"Well, no, actually not, but I could have paid you sometime, Barb. I'm not always broke."

"Well, I'm sorry," she said. "I got a good offer and I took it. I know you think I'm a money-grubber, but I have to think about next year. Of course, Dad is going to pay my tuition and board and room and all that, but a person wants to have a little extra. You never seem to think beyond the middle of next week."

"If that far," I said. "This is true, and we are basically incompatible. Let's get a divorce, or at least change the subject."

Barbara cheered up immediately, as I had known she would. I was actually still furious, but since I would have to spend at least another hour socializing, I didn't want to push things from bad to worse in the first five minutes.

"You're really sweet, Jill," she said.

"I couldn't agree more. Now tell me something I don't already know."

Barbara leaned back against the end of her bed, ready for the old girlish confidences. "Actually," she said, "I've been dying to tell you where I went Saturday night. You know Sean?"

I nodded, picturing a head of curly blond hair about six

and a half feet off the ground and a brain the size of a walnut.

"Well, Sean took me to an Iranian nightclub," she went on. "Can you believe it? I didn't even know they had nightclubs."

"That was very brave of him," I said gravely.

"Yes. Well, actually it was a double date," Barbara said, and now, for some unaccountable reason, she began to look uncomfortable again. "We went with Simmy Simpson, and her date was Iranian, so we had someone to show us the ropes."

I confess to a fleeting moment of panic, but it was soon past. There might be dark patches in Shaheen's life, but Simmy was certainly not one of them.

"Hassan Marubian," she went on. "Know him?"

"Short, dark, slightly moth-eaten?"

"He's really very nice," she said, "and disgustingly rich. We had bottles and bottles of champagne. They just kept appearing as if by magic. You would have had a musical fit, I suppose. They played this Iranian rock, but it's really sort of neat once you get used to it. Romantic. Good for dancing. We danced a lot. I didn't know Iranians went in for that sort of thing."

"That depends," I said. "A lot of the rich ones do and the ones who aren't very religious. Your pal Marubian is almost certainly a Christian, by the way. That's an Armenian name. Not that it makes much difference. I believe they can be very strict too, or not, as the case may be. Anyway, Iranians like to have a good time as much as anyone else, and they aren't severe like the Arabs."

"Before I came here, I thought they were all the same," Barbara said.

"Well, so did I," I said. "Live and learn. Travel is broadening. So what else did you do besides dance and guzzle indecent amounts of champagne?"

"Oh, we talked a lot. You know how people do when they're sitting around drinking. Except it was very noisy, and I couldn't hear everything that was said very well. That's why I wonder if I should repeat any of it. You know. I could have gotten it all wrong."

"Gotten what all wrong?" I said crossly. "I didn't even ask you what you talked about, and with that trio of great brains I doubt if I'd want to know."

"Oh yes you would," Barbara said, stung out of her evasiveness. "Because one of the things we talked about was your friend Shaheen, and how he was sleeping with an American girl last year when he was only sixteen. And then she went back to the States very suddenly for some reason that was never explained."

I looked at Barbara with her pretty face red beneath its halo of artfully frizzy dark hair and at the familiar room where we had spent so many hours, and I didn't see a thing. It was as if I had been suddenly struck blind, but not, fortunately, dumb. My tongue came to my rescue and I said the first thing that came into my head. "Sixteen?" I said. "You make it sound as if he had crawled out of the cradle to do the deed. Surely it would make a better story if he'd been twelve?"

"You don't believe me?" she asked.

"Of course I believe you heard what you say you heard," I said. "Even through the thunderous fizzing of champagne glasses, I'm sure the message came through loud and clear. But, in the first place, I make it a point not to believe every little piece of gossip I hear, and in the second place, so what?"

"So what? You mean you don't care?"

"Why should I care?" I said. I had recovered my composure by now, and what went on inside was my own business. Besides, I was beginning to talk some sense into my own head. "For one thing," I went on, "Shaheen and I are only very good friends, as I have told you repeatedly. For another thing, Shaheen is a man, and whatever you may think of my worldly sophistication, I am bored to tears with boys. I also object to your tone of moral indignation. It's not as if Shaheen were a native who molested a missionary. I, frankly, have never thought of my Iranian friends in quite that way."

"That's not fair," Barbara cried. "I didn't mean anything of the kind. I was only telling you something I thought you ought to know because I'm your friend. I see I made a mistake. Excuse me."

"People are always telling other people things for their own good," I said. "It must be one of the major causes of the world's problems."

At this point we heard the front door slam and James, loud and cheery, saying, "Hi. Where's my sis?"

"You know where she is, silly," Marjorie's voice said. "Take your boots off, James, like a good boy, and I'll give you some more cookies and cocoa."

I got up hastily, seeing an easy way out of this ghastly conversation. "James is here," I said unnecessarily. "He'll be wanting to go home."

Barbara looked as if she wanted to cry. "Don't go yet, Jill," she said. "I'm really sorry. I can't think what got into me to trot out all that stupid gossip."

I stood looking down at her for a moment, torn between rage and regret. "Can't you?" I said. "Well, we all make mistakes. And look, Barb, it really doesn't matter, you know. So let's forget it."

She still looked stricken, but she got up and trailed forlornly after me into the kitchen where James, bootless, was starting on another round of winter refreshments.

"Hey, Jill, I've got a great idea," he said. "Why don't we call Dad at the office and get him to stop for us on his way home? We can put the sled in the trunk and not have to climb all that way."

This horrible proposal was all too logical, and I could have killed him since it would mean at least another two hours of the Enrights. "We can't, Jamie," I said quickly. "It's only four o'clock. He couldn't get here before six, and I really have to practice before dinner."

James must have caught the note of desperation in my voice for he shrugged philosophically and said, "All right, all right, we'll hoof it, although you know how deeply I loathe exercise."

"I do, and I appreciate it," I said. "I'll remember you in my will."

"May you expire soon from too much mountain climbing," my brother said without rancor.

"My, Jill, you certainly are taking your music seriously these days," Marjorie said, with her usual gift for underlining that which is best left alone.

"I'm trying to," I said politely and started to pull my boots on. "Come, dear brother. We may as well get it over with."

James, having decided to be noble, slid off his stool and got back into his winter clothes without complaint. Freedom was at hand, and I felt suddenly sorry for Barbara. "Come up to our place before the snow melts," I said. "Then you can slide home. It's ever so much better to live at the bottom for this kind of socializing."

"Haven't got a sled," she said, "but thanks anyway."

"Well, maybe we can work out a way for you to borrow ours and have somebody drive it home." I was determined now to be cordial, just as if the whole nasty scene had been my fault, but all I got was a wan smile for my pains.

Marjorie was looking scandalized. "I don't think sledding alone in Tehran would be such a brilliant idea for a girl, Jill," she said.

"That's a point," I said, slapping James on the back. "I forgot I had a big he-man to escort me through the wilds of Shemiran. Well, cheers, everybody. We'll work something out, and thanks for all the goodies."

Once we were safely out the door, James said, "So what was that all about? You looked as if there was poison in the cocoa."

"That's about the way I felt," I said, feeling suddenly depressed all over again. I had a rash desire to tell James everything that had passed between me and Barbara that afternoon and how I felt about it, but I knew better. He was a very bright and sensitive kid, but he just hadn't lived long enough. There was, in fact, no one I could talk to except my father, and he, perhaps, had lived a bit too long. "Barbara and I just aren't getting along as well as we used to," I added. "We've grown apart, and we spent the time sniping at each other. It's upsetting when you've been so close to someone."

"She always was a dumb broad," James said unsympathetically. "Like mother, like daughter. You let all those books fool you. Anybody can read."

I laughed. This ridiculous and unfair statement had made me feel much better. "That's just your point of view," I said, "and Barbara isn't really at all stupid, you know, just staggeringly opaque sometimes. Let's forget the whole pack of them."

"Fine with me," he said. "Expatriate friends aren't all they might be. You know what I miss from home? Friends.

We're lucky we've got a good family, otherwise all this trekking around would be a drag."

I peered anxiously at my brother's face in the deepening twilight. "Are you homesick, Jamie?" I asked.

"Who, me?" He seemed surprised. "I think this place is neat, don't you?"

"Yes," I said. "I do."

"Besides," James went on, "you have a really great, close friend, haven't you?"

My astonishment deepened. Others might tease and insinuate, but my eleven-year-old brother could see that at least one of the things Shaheen was to me was a really great, close friend. I reached out with the arm that wasn't pulling the sled and gave him a quick squeeze from which he shied only slightly. "That's right," I said, "and I hope you get one too before we're through."

"Not your kind, I devoutly hope," James said, and we trudged on in amicable silence.

It had turned very cold with the coming of night, and we moved upward through a tunnel of snow, snow under our feet, snow piled against the garden walls. Over the walls the white treetops glowed softly in the warm light spilling from windows which gave upon the secret gardens of Tehran. The sky had cleared, and before us the mountains reared ghostly heads against the first stars.

Slowly now, as the stars gathered, the petty turmoil of the day faded from my mind, leaving behind only what was bright and clean and simple. I said to myself: I love Shaheen. It doesn't matter how others see it or even how he sees it. This is my secret, my joy, and my strength. Against this fact I will order the universe.

Chapter 14

The following morning I woke with the feeling that I would not survive the day if I didn't see Shaheen. This was not a new sensation, but it did seem that by calling my state by its true name, I had intensified all the symptoms. It was like feeling only mildly sick until you take your temperature and find that it is one hundred and four. The remaining week of the Christmas vacation stretched before me into eternity.

After breakfast and half an hour of gazing at my books in the hope that one of them would interest me, I went to the phone. It goes without saying that Shaheen was not at home, nor were any of the other English-speaking members of the household. I don't know which granny answered my call, but she had either a strong regional accent or no teeth or both. However, her attitude toward foreign girls who telephoned her grandson was clear. Resolving never to call that particular number again, I crawled back to my room, switched on my miserable cassette machine, and prepared to endure the rest of the day in passive suffering.

At three o'clock Shaheen called me. "Hi," he said, "I think I've found the right rug for you. May I bring it out?"

It had been more than a month since we had talked about a remedy for our bare floor, so I had filed the whole rug question under "Persian Promises" and forgotten all about it. "You've got what?" I said. "Good Lord, Shaheen, I didn't know you were really going through with that mad scheme. Is it your father's? Doesn't he mind?"

"He's been helping me look," Shaheen said. "Even with his stock it took a while to find one that would do something for your appalling furniture. Now please be a dear girl and tell me if you're busy. I don't want to load the damn thing unless you will be on hand to give it a home."

"Load it?" I asked. "Load it as opposed to put it in the car?"

"Be sensible," Shaheen said. "You've seen my car, and you've seen your floor. Now, shall I come?"

"Absolutely come," I said, giving up on the rug and concentrating on more important issues. "I'm expiring of boredom. Come for dinner. I can't think of a better opportunity."

"I don't know about that," he said.

"I do. Come on, Shaheen. You can't avoid my parents forever. They're really quite agreeable."

"All right, then. Thanks, Jill. Don't kill the fatted calf or whatever it is you people do."

"And stop pretending to be so ignorant of American households," I said. "If you're going to play the simple boy from the mountains, you need to take acting lessons."

"I thought I had you fooled," he said. "Well, see you later then. What time? Six, seven, eight?"

"Make it six," I said. "We don't have to eat instantly or even soon. Come when you like."

"Six it is," he said, and hung up.

I turned to see my mother standing in the doorway to the kitchen and regarding me with consternation. "Jill, did I just hear you invite someone to dinner, or am I really losing my mind at last?"

"Shaheen," I said. "I'm sorry. I know I should have asked, but if I had hesitated even a second, the fish would have been off the hook."

"I haven't been able to shop in days," she said. "There's not a morsel in the house to eat."

"What were we going to have?"

"Canned Iranian hot dogs," she said, vindictively.

"I don't believe you," I said. "Let's see what's in the freezer."

She followed me back into the kitchen, still looking rebellious, and watched while I prodded the depths of our enormous freezer. "Frozen cherries," I said, "spinach, and a large block of something that has to be squid."

"Fine," my mother said., "I'll teach you to plan an important dinner without asking me."

I laughed. "You'll think of something," I said. "I have perfect faith. Meanwhile I'll go down the hill and find some decent vegetables and fresh *barbari*."

"You'll be sorry," Mum said, but her voice came muffled from the inside of the freezer, and I knew the creative process was already at work as I went for my coat and boots.

For some reason the apprehensions I had once felt about having Shaheen visit us had vanished. So, not surprisingly, had my earlier case of the blues. I felt festive and full of energy. Then I remembered the original purpose of his call and went back to the kitchen. "There's something I ought to tell you," I said. "Shaheen is lending us what I suspect is a rather large carpet."

"A carpet?" my mother said, juggling a package of something frozen in each hand. "Won't one carpet look rather strange? I should think we needed five or six, which is one reason I've never tried to solve the problem."

"I'm afraid this one will be adequate," I said.

I spent the next hour tramping from one tiny fruit and vegetable stall to another through the snowy streets of our neighborhood. Their offerings seemed more than usually bleak, but I was in no mood to be discouraged. Home again, I managed to use up some more time by setting and resetting the table, pushing our four pieces of furniture around, and general fidgeting. At around five Ali came out of his room yawning and stretching from his afternoon nap.

"Oh, Ali," I said casually in Farsi. "We are having a guest to dinner, my friend from school."

"MG Irani?" he asked with interest.

"Yes, the Irani with the MG," I said, refusing to switch languages. "Please try to be courteous. He comes from a very good family. *Bazaari*. Rich."

"Tehrani good no," Ali said, revealing a new layer of prejudice.

"Really?" I said. "Strange. I have heard the same about people from your province."

"Stop it, you two," my mother called from the kitchen. "Ali, I need you. Come. *Bia inja*, please." And Ali went.

At last it was nearly six, and I went to the window to gaze out into the white stillness of our little street.

Shaheen and my father arrived at the same moment. This was a good thing considering the size of the rug. I ran to the door and stood there laughing at the sight of the MG, which was almost invisible under the huge roll stretched lengthwise on its roof. The fact that the little car had made it up the icy slope of Asef with such a burden was a tribute to British engineering. Shaheen got out looking a trifle pale. He and my father shook hands ceremoniously and started fumbling with the ropes that secured the rug. Then they carried it into the house and dropped it in the largest empty space. All of this activity broke the ice, and they were full of male camaraderie as they stripped off their gloves and winter coats. My father, however, was still in the dark as to the reason for all his effort. "My God, Jill," he said, contemplating the thing on the floor, "what's happened? Did we win a lottery?"

"Shaheen thought we needed a little something on the floor," I said, "so he's lending us a rug. Hurry up. Unroll it. I can't wait."

My mother and Ali had appeared from the kitchen by now and James from his room. They all stood around open-mouthed as the two men unrolled what seemed to me to be the biggest and most ravishingly beautiful Persian carpet I had ever seen.

"The blues and purples are hard to find," Shaheen said, matter of factly. "That's what took me so long, but I think this does the job, don't you, Jill?"

I nodded mutely. There seemed to be a thousand shades of blue and violet woven into the intricate designs, and it made our furniture look, if not distinguished, at least as if it belonged to the room.

"It's beautiful," my mother said from across the rug. "Thank you so much, Shaheen, and welcome to our previously humble home."

Shaheen sprinted across to shake her hand. "I'm so happy to be here," he said, and I could see her melt still further under his dazzling smile.

He turned, laughing, to the rest of us. "You know, it's going to be inconvenient if you don't walk on it," he said. "It's rather a long way around."

James was the first. He crawled rather than walked to the

94

center of the rug and lay down on his back with a blissful expression. I joined him sitting down. "That solves the problem of the furniture," I said. "Now we can throw it out."

"The question is," my mother said, "shall we put the furniture on the rug, which seems rather a shame, or shall we leave the rug here in solitary splendor and admire it from the furniture, if you know what I mean?"

"Leave it alone," James said, rolling over several times.

"This is a problem I feel could better be solved with drinks in our hands," my father said. "Vodka or wine or something less sinful, Shaheen?"

"Wine," I think," Shaheen said. "Vodka might impair my judgment in this serious matter."

I am not going to give you a blow-by-blow account of our dinner from drinks through dessert. My mother, excavating below the frozen squid, had found a real treasure lying flat on the bottom of the freezer; five Dover soles had somehow made their way from the English Channel to honor Shaheen in Tehran. The meal was fun as well as delicious, and any fears I might have had about Shaheen and my family getting along were soon dispelled. They jabbered away like old friends about everything but politics, an omission for which I was not sure whether to be glad or sorry. Neither Shaheen nor my father, however, had any intention of neglecting such a fascinating topic. They were merely biding their time.

"Jill tells me you are doing some teaching," Shaheen said with deceptive innocence when we had finally finished dinner and settled ourselves in the depths of the controversial chairs, a second bottle of wine open on the coffee table in front of us.

"And that's about all I'm doing," Dad said, "but it turns out to be quite enough to occupy my time. As you may know, I started out trying to drag the oil company kicking and screaming into the twentieth century; but I ended up doing all the kicking and screaming myself. They were simply not interested, although that was the job I was hired to do. They would rather, just for example, burn off all the natural gas that comes up out of the ground instead of injecting it back into the wells to force out more oil, something we have known how to do for donkey's years. Have you seen the refineries at night down around Abadan?" Shaheen shook his head. "They light up the sky for miles around in the most beautiful display of conspicuous waste that one could hope to see. That's just one thing we could have started to fix. But no, why bother? There seems to be so much oil. When one well gets low, they just drill another."

"No imagination. No thought for the future," Shaheen said.

"The management of Naft Melli is old," my father said, "old and corrupt and comfortable. But the shah is always full of bright ideas, and he thinks hiring a lot of foreign experts will make his dreams come true in some magical way; so the experts are hired (after all, there's no shortage of money), and then systematically frustrated into the ground."

"Except for the electronic surveillance experts," Shaheen said. "They get plenty of interesting and rewarding work to do making their little gadgets for SAVAK to use; but I suppose the rest of you — the ones who would really like to do something constructive for this thankless country — get pretty sick of it all."

"Believe me, I nearly packed up my family and went home," Dad said, "which would have been a shame as it turned out. Then some of the young engineers started asking me questions, and there is nothing I like better than answering questions, usually at great length and in overwhelming detail. I asked the directors if I could give some courses in my abundant spare time, and they agreed. So here we are, four months later and everybody happy."

"Everybody?" Shaheen said softly.

My father looked uncomfortable. "Well, not quite everybody," he admitted. "In fact, maybe not anybody completely. The management is beginning to think that my courses are a focus of subversion, since it is rumored that we sometimes discuss subjects other than engineering. As for the students, the more they learn, the more miserable they become."

"Oh yes?" Shaheen said. "I should think they would be delighted."

"They are delighted to be learning, but they don't know what they're going to do with their new knowledge. You know yourself that really bright people are not wanted. Perhaps they are perceived to be a threat. I don't know about that, but I do know that I can turn out a brilliant young engineer, and he will be given a clipboard and a white smock and put to reading gages in a refinery without any prospect of ever doing anything more interesting. The alternative, I fear, is all too obvious."

"America," Shaheen said bitterly.,

My father nodded. "America, Europe, even England. Unless there is a drastic change in attitude toward these young men and women, Iran is going to lose eighty percent of them, and Iran's loss will be our gain."

Shaheen leaned forward, his eyes blazing. "They must stay! They must stay and make a new society — one in which they can do their best work and do it for their own country."

My father spread his hands in a gesture of futility. "You know what the obstacles are," he said.

"The obstacles will be removed," Shaheen said, "by force

if necessary. Once the shah and his corrupt bureaucrats are gone, we can get something done in this country. But the intellectuals must not run away now when we need them most."

"You are too few," my father said. "Think, lad; how many of you are there to man the barricades against the army and the riot police?"

"The army is not so fond of the shah as you may think," Shaheen answered. "Besides, we have other, more powerful allies. The bazaari hate the regime for their own, selfish financial reasons. The mullahs hate it even more. When the shah took their lands to give to the peasants during the White Revolution, he left the peasants as miserable as ever since they had nothing to farm with — no seed, no machines, no transportation — and he made deadly enemies of the mullahs. They began plotting to get rid of the Pahlavis and using the thousands of mosques all over Iran as revolutionary cells. Since the poor are devout and go often to worship, we have a fantastic communications network already in place. The Ayatollah Khomeini has only to sneeze in Iraq, and a day later the noses of the faithful are twitching all over Iran."

"I know he has a tremendous following," my father said.

"He is the kind of leader who only comes along once in a century," Shaheen said. "And we have him now when we need him. Never mind that he is an old-fashioned religious conservative. He is a great power for good, and the people will follow him to the death."

My father gazed anxiously at Shaheen. Finally he said, "This is not the first time I have heard of such an alliance, and believe me, every time I hear of it, I am filled with greater consternation. You are proposing to tear down a stable, if odious, government with a coalition of leftist intellectuals, conservative merchants and Stone Age reactionaries from the religious establishment. What in hell do you think you're going to have when you get through?"

"A mess," I said, and was rewarded with a baleful look from Shaheen.

"The mullahs aren't so bad," he said, "and they have tremendous, charismatic power. They appeal to the people's love of traditional values — to what they see as old virtues which are being submerged by Western ways."

"Things like keeping women in the home, all wrapped up in chadors," I said, wondering why I felt so inspired to be the devil's advocate.

Shaheen turned on me. "The shah tried to take the women out of their chadors," he said, "and where did it get him? A lot of Iranian women equate the chador with virtue, and they should have as much right to wear it as women like you have to go around in jeans. You don't know enough yet, Jill, about what the Iranian people are like and what they want. You couldn't possibly in this length of time."

"Are you sure you do, Shaheen?" my father asked quietly.

For a moment Shaheen said nothing. He was looking at us in a strange, calm way. The anger had drained out of his face, but the passion was still there, and his voice shook slightly. "Life, liberty, and the pursuit of happiness," he said. "Isn't that the way it goes? The Iranian people don't want anything more unreasonable than any people anywhere. And if liberty for some means wearing a chador and praying five times a day, I am sure you would be among the first to defend them."

"I only hope that it all turns out for the good," my father said heavily. "I mistrust all fundamentalist religions, and I don't have to know much about Islam to know that if you let a pack of mullahs or priests or even Protestant ministers get the upper hand, Lady Liberty will have to go looking for another revolution. So watch the boys in the long robes, Shaheen. You might do better without them."

"We can't move an inch without them, and you know it," Shaheen said. "But I don't see the threat. Many Iranians are very religious, but they don't want to turn back the clock. Look at us. We enjoy the good things in life too much." He was smiling now, and he lifted his glass full of golden Iranian wine. "A loaf of bread, a jug of wine, and thou." For a moment the black eyes flashed mockingly in my direction. "We're not a bunch of bloody, dismal Arabs, you know."

My father laughed and raised his glass. "To the Iranian character in all its complexities," he said, "and to your future, Shaheen."

The future has arrived as it always does no matter how much we long to hold it back, and I remember that conversation in Tehran with a mixture of astonishment and grief. How could the foreign visitor have been so right and the native son so wrong? I suppose that those who are deeply involved in great events can never see so clearly as those who stand even a short distance away. My father's comments were prophetic; but I think they arose more out of his own feelings about many things — about democracy and violence and ideological tyranny — than from a factual knowledge of the situation. Facts in those days were few, and many issues were obscured by the looming figure of the shah. Today the thing my father feared has come to pass and has taken a form more terrible than our worst imaginings. Iran has passed from a vision of liberty into a night of medieval terror, and the dark robes of the mullahs shadow our dreams.

I am glad that the future was hidden from us — glad that we could sit there in a circle of warmth talking as we did, our thoughts moving on currents of hope and fear, anger and laughter, floating on the black tide of things to come as if in a small vessel filled with the light of our common humanity.

Shaheen left that night at a flatteringly late hour. After he had gone, the three of us stood around cautiously on the new rug finishing our wine and talking. My mother sighed. "Well, if you ever get tired of him, Jill, be sure to let me know."

"I'm afraid there are others standing in line at school," I said. "I've been thinking of hiring a taster for all my food and drink."

"He's very bright," my father said. "I hope he finds something worthwhile to do. Where is he going next year?"

"To Brown to study city planning so he can take Tehran apart and put it back together again after the revolution," I said, "but, of course, it all depends . . . on a lot of things . . ." My voice trailed away, and a wing of shadow brushed once more through the bright room.

"On whether the revolution comes first, and he feels he has to stay," my father finished for me, and I nodded miserably.

"In November he was sure it had come," I said, "when the students were killed after the poetry readings. And other things have happened since, but not so bad — not enough to really set off an explosion. Now I keep hoping for more delay. If only he will leave in one of these quiet times and not be able to get back. Let someone else do the shooting."

"He wouldn't like that, you know," Dad said gently. "But I wouldn't worry too much. This time of uneasy stability may last for years. The shah is trying to show everybody that he's really not such a bad guy after all — muzzling SAVAK, letting prisoners out, putting forth a rash of pleasant-sounding new social programs. This should at least keep our young friends below the boiling point."

"Well, I certainly hope so," my mother said. "I am really beginning to like it here, and I can't wait to see what will come up in the garden this spring. I may even plant some things myself."

I looked at her affectionately. It was like her to be planning a garden three days after Christmas. "That will be lovely," I said, and suddenly in my mind a glorious succession of days stretched ahead — days full of sun and snow and flowers, days of music and of love.

Chapter 15

School began, and I regarded its onset with mixed feelings. Like many seniors, I was beginning to be rather bored with it all, but going to school meant seeing Shaheen every day, and this tipped the scales in favor of education.

The bus came for us at six forty-five — a chilly time in the foothills of the Alborz Mountains in January. It was often late, but sometimes early, so that we stood muffled to the ears on Asef wondering how long it would be or if we had already missed it. Yet these were mornings I shall never forget, for a winter dawn in Shemiran is overwhelmingly beautiful. Before sunrise the sky is a pale, transparent green. Against it the white mountains stand wrapped in silence — majestic, remote, yet so near one feels dwarfed by their enormous presence. Slowly they take on color from the still invisible sun, and then far away in the East, suddenly, the single cone of Damavand blazes with the first light of day. Numb with cold and a sense of awe, we waited for the unmistakable sounds of our bus, the clank of chains, the grinding of gears, the groan of an overworked engine. It arrived

103

like a spacecraft from another world, a capsule of light and noise crawling among the craters of the moon.

At school the slow progression of classes was brightened by an hour of band every day. The Community School band was surprisingly good considering its rather catch-as-catch-can instrumentation. We were fortunate in not having to waste a third of our time on the football field, and in our enthusiastic young conductor, whom everyone adored. Mr. Perenyi drove us with a kind of cheerful ruthlessness that produced surprisingly excellent results. This was just as well, since I doubt that Shaheen would have bothered with a less rewarding group. He was fairly scornful as it was, but every musician needs a place to play, and amateur orchestras were not numerous in Tehran. I, for my part, loved every minute of it and had from the beginning.

After band I had the only class I really liked, an advanced placement English course which included both writing and reading poetry as well as a lot of delightfully random conversation with people who shared my interests. Then, almost without fail, came an hour of even more satisfying talk in the cozy confines of the green MG.

During the last few days of the vacation Shaheen had decided to supplement his mustache with a full beard, and I sat in the car casting furtive glances at him and wondering what the effect was going to be once the worst was over. Happily, for an Iranian the villainous stage is brief. They can pretty much grow beards and shave them off at will without worrying about the interim. At the moment, however, about three days into the project, he looked like a dangerous criminal or, I thought uneasily, an urban guerrilla. This effect was offset by his clothes, in this case a pair of faded-to-perfection jeans and an Icelandic sweater in wonderful shades of brown and cream.

"I wonder if I am going to like it," I said, when one of my stares brought a quizzical smile in return.

"Sure you will," Shaheen said. "It will be *kheili* sexy."

I laughed. This was the inevitable Iranian description of certain well-loved American films which were still to be seen in the capital. "Well, just don't go completely into the bush," I said. "It would make me feel insecure not to be able to see your expressions."

"*Cherâ?*" he asked mockingly, then, "Don't worry. Something neat and Elizabethan was more what I had in mind."

We were sitting in an impossible snarl of traffic on Bazaarjomehri, the wide but not nearly wide enough avenue that runs along the north side of the Bazaar Bozorg and is one of several unsatisfactory ways of getting from east to west in downtown Tehran. I could see why Shaheen always said that covering the relatively short distance from school to his house was a major undertaking, and this was precisely what we were attempting to do. Finally I was to be introduced to the Rohani household, and I was jumpy as a cat. The main idea was to play some duets, but Shaheen warned me it would be rather more complicated than that.

"What exactly do you mean by more complicated?" I asked. "I presume I will meet some members of your family. That strikes me as normal and not too alarming."

"There will be tea," Shaheen said with gloomy satisfaction, "and biscuits and fruit and nuts. With any sort of luck there won't be too many people, and we will be able to get away after a while."

"My God," I said. "You shouldn't have told your mother I was coming."

"Oh it's not for you," he answered. "The process is more or less continuous, particularly in the late afternoon."

"It sounds very agreeable," I said. "Warm, sociable."

"It's all of that, and it is also excruciatingly boring," Shaheen said, changing gears savagely and shooting ahead into a space which had miraculously opened up in front of us.

Staring down the confused lanes of Bazaarjomehri, I saw that for some reason the traffic had loosened up. Once past the bazaar, it would not take long to reach our goal. I glanced apprehensively at my carefully chosen clothes — gray flannel slacks and a navy shetland sweater — modest, casual, excellent quality. "Am I wearing the right thing?" I asked, "or doesn't it matter?"

"You're fine," he said. "So long as it isn't a bikini or spangled tights or something of that sort, it hardly matters. In a sense anything you wore would be right, because all the ladies will be interested in it, and anything you wore would be wrong because it will be the subject of elaborate criticism."

"Stop the car," I said, only half in jest. "I'm going to walk home."

"Don't worry," he said. "I'm only teasing about the clothes. Everyone will be enormously kind, and after a round of goodies, we'll break away and go do our own thing. Here, have a cigarette. You're all in a stew."

I took a cigarette from his pack and he lit it for me with his lighter, his long fingers brushing mine as they always did in a seemingly accidental caress. I felt immediately relaxed and reassured, though I couldn't help thinking how much better yet would be a good, hearty squeeze.

Shaheen's house was in a tree-lined street that was crammed with Mercedes of various sizes and BMWs, the Iranian lady's car. He found a gap between two gleaming monsters and parked the MG. Before us loomed a battered, brown wall with a wooden gate that sagged on its hinges. Behind the wall more huge trees shaded the house, a two-

106

story structure built around a courtyard. Here there was a fountain, which was playing even now in the middle of winter. It looked chilly and forlorn, but I could guess at summer splendors from the many rose bushes in formal plantings around its basin. They had been cropped short for the cold weather, but one still bore a blood-red rose. Shaheen strolled over to the fountain. "It's beautiful here in the summer," he said. "We sit outside in the evenings, here by the fountain or on the roof when it's hot. Before the air got so bad you could see the stars and even the mountains at dusk or in the moonlight. Now, well, we still have the trees; and the roses go on blooming, God knows how." His face, darkened by the new beard, was pensive and a little sad. "The Persian rose," he said, cupping the bright flower for a moment in his hand. "What a brave and foolhardy thing it is."

I looked at him silently, and he gazed back with somber, dark eyes. Then he smiled and turned toward the house. "Come," he said. "We must brave the party and get to our music." And I followed him obediently across the garden, lugging my horn in one hand and wishing I were almost any place but here.

Before Shaheen could open the door, it was opened for us by what seemed to be a very old lady in a black chador. (I later learned that she was only around sixty, the younger of the two grandmothers.) Shaheen introduced her quickly in Farsi, and I took the wrinkled little hand that had crept out of the black draperies and murmured, "*Salaam, Khanoum. Hal-e-shoma?*" She gave me a wonderful smile and greeted me in turn in a voice and accent I immediately recognized. This gentle creature was the terrifying old witch I had talked to on the telephone.

We left our horns in the hall and followed her into a room which seemed to be full of people all talking at once. They

107

were of both sexes and every age, from a child of about two who sat under the tea table with a cookie in each fist to the great grandmother huddled on a bench in a corner with only her nose and her sharp, black eyes peeping out from the folds of her chador. All the other women were in European dress, although some, I knew, would don chadors when they left the house. The men wore dark suits and ties and shiny Italian shoes with pointed toes.

The room was rather sparsely furnished, perhaps to make room for the daily horde of visitors, but I saw, to my delight, a group of chairs which for sheer awfulness easily rivaled our lavender living room suite. The difference, of course, was in the floor covering. The Rohani salon was wall-to-wall Persian rugs. They lapped the sides of the room in waves of color and overlapped each other in a profusion that was at once confusing and incredibly rich. All of this magnificence was illuminated by an enormous crystal chandelier.

Silence fell as we made our entrance, and I felt my Farsi run out of my mind like water down a drain, leaving not a drop behind. Shaheen said, "Come, you must meet everyone." Then as he took me around the room, the chatter gradually resumed, and I felt my confidence seeping back. It was not, after all, very difficult to get through the conventional greetings which, by now, I knew backward and forward. This seemed to be all that was required.

The first person was a beautiful woman in her thirties whose red hair looked almost natural. She was wearing jeans and a flannel shirt, and her smile was open and sunny. "Ashraf, my favorite aunt," Shaheen said, and she greeted me in slow, clear Farsi as if she, too, had some experience of the terrors of socializing in a foreign language.

Shaheen's father was, somewhat to my relief, not present, this being a busy time of day in the bazaar. His mother, however, was very much in evidence. She was a thin, elegant woman whose nervous gestures set the gold bangles clashing on her delicate wrists as she talked first to one guest, then to another. A recent tan set off the whiteness of her teeth but did little to complement her hair which, like that of so many upper-class Iranian women, had been reddened with henna. She greeted me effusively in the same polished English I had heard on the phone, but I felt her small, sharp eyes were taking in every detail of my person and finding most of them wanting. Probably hates my guts on general principles, I thought. That she adored her only son was clear, but then, everyone else in the room seemed to feel the same.

When the last introduction had been performed, Shaheen left me to my own devices and began to circulate on his own, spreading his charm in all directions. A cup of tea was thrust into my hand; then a huge plate of sweets appeared from the other side. I studied the beautiful mound of golden nests and curls and knots trying to remember which ones had rose water and which not. This was a distinction which made all the difference between delicious and repellent to my foreign palate. Probably bakers had their own styles, so that a bow-knot from Tajrish might be flavored like a curlicue from South Tehran. I took a chance and got rose water.

Now I felt a slight bumping at my elbow and turned to see a little girl straining under the weight of a huge fruit platter and looking up at me with Shaheen's dark eyes. "Hello, Jill. I am Shams. How are you? Do you want some fruit?" she said all in a rush as if to get this carefully rehearsed English lesson over as quickly as possible. I smiled down at her. She was a pocket edition of the classic Persian beauty, with straight, black brows almost meeting at the top of an already promising nose and dark hair loose down her back. "I am happy to meet you," I said slowly. "You must be Shaheen's sister."

"And you are his girl friend," Shams said, looking me up and down. "Your hair is beautiful," she concluded as a result of this examination.

To hide my confusion I bent over and offered to take the platter. "That must be heavy," I said in Farsi. "Let me put it on the table, and then I will take something."

My reward for this linguistic triumph was a storm of giggles which Shams tried politely to stifle with her hand. "You speak funny," she gasped finally.

"So do you," I said and relieved her of the platter.

"I am English in school," Shams said.

"I am *studying* English in school," I corrected automatically. "Do you like English?"

Shams considered this gambit with more attention than it deserved. "I like English," she said at last, "and I like you, but . . ." She stopped and looked hopefully at me.

"I really can understand Farsi," I said, switching languages again. "Just speak slowly."

"But I think it is very silly to spend so much time studying something we are not going to use," she continued with obvious relief at having returned to a language in which she could chatter.

"*Cherá?* English is a very useful language."

"It is useful now," Shams explained, "but when we have made all the Americans go home, it will not be useful any more."

I looked sadly around the cheerful, crowded room and over to where Shaheen was talking to one of the men. "But I don't want to go home, Shams."

She gave me a long, thoughtful look. Then she said,

"Well, you can stay, Jill. Perhaps you will marry Shaheen and become an Iranian."

I was saved from having to respond to this suggestion by the arrival of another sister. Out of the frying pan into the fire, as it turned out, but for the moment I was glad of the diversion. Nineteen-year-old Laleh came into the room like a gust of wind, slamming the door, dumping a heavy knapsack of books under the tea table. She was a tall, robust girl with a mass of unruly curls framing a vivid face. I knew that she was doing her military service as a member of the literacy corps, commuting every day in a dilapidated bus to a village south of Tehran where she taught the children to read and write. Pausing only to snatch a cookie from the tray, Laleh strode over to Shaheen, and they embraced as if they hadn't seen each other for years. Next she greeted her mother and her two grandmothers politely but hastily, as if she had little time for old-fashioned amenities, and turned back to Shaheen. I wondered when either of them would get around to me and decided that I could stand to wait.

"That's Laleh," Shams told me. "She's a teacher. She wants to be a lawyer, but she didn't make up her mind fast enough so the army got her. Now she has to teach little kids their *alef-bey* for two years before she can go to university."

"Too bad," I said. "What about you? I suppose you won't make the same mistake."

Shams gave me a slightly dreamy look. "I am a poet," she said, "so it could be complicated except that by the time I am ready for university, everything will be different. I won't have to do military service for the shah."

I was still contemplating this spate of information and trying to frame a sensible comment in Farsi when the brother and sister bore down on me, Shaheen in the lead.

111

"Jill," he cried. "Here's my sister, Laleh. I've told you about her."

His enthusiasm was infectious, but Laleh was immune. She extended her hand coolly and said in flawless but frigid English, "How do you do? I am so pleased to meet you."

I was immediately plunged into an abyss of shyness. What does one say to such a greeting from a contemporary? I said, "How do you do?" in return, and let it go at that.

Laleh, however, seemed to feel that something more was required, if only for her brother's sake. "I understand you are also a musician," she said.

"I play the horn," I said, "like Shaheen. In fact, that's how we met — in the band at school." This sounded too apologetic, so I made it worse by adding, "but, of course, you already know about all that."

"Yes," Laleh said, "it has been so nice for him to know someone who could share his musical interests. Unfortunately, few Iranians care for Western instruments."

There were several interpretations I could have put on this remark if her tone of voice had left me any choice. "That's all right," I said sweetly. "It will probably do him no harm to know one American musician."

"Almost certainly not," she said with a shrug which dismissed me as almost certainly harmless.

Shaheen was looking at us with consternation. It was the first time I had seen him at a loss for words, and this might have been gratifying if I hadn't so badly needed some support. Obviously I was going to have to get out of this conversation by myself. "Speaking of music," I said firmly, "if we're going to play duets, we'd better get at it. I have a paper to write tonight, and it's getting late."

"Please don't let me stand in your way," Laleh said.

"Goodbye, Jill. See you later, Shaheen," and, flashing a brilliant smile in our general direction, she moved back into the crowd of friends and relatives.

"Let's go then," Shaheen said resignedly. "Don't try to say goodbye to anybody. You can do the important ones when you go home."

As I turned toward the door, I saw that Shams was still at my side. Probably she had been there all along like a little shadow. "Here's an important one I'll say goodbye to now, because I wouldn't want to miss her," I said. "*Khoda hafez,* Shams. I hope we can have another talk soon, and thank you for making me feel so welcome."

"*Khoda hafez,* Jill," she replied, "and don't mind Laleh. She's really very nice when you get to know her."

"I'm sure she is," I said. "Perhaps I will get to know her someday, but I feel as if I know you now, and I'm very happy that I do."

She gave a little wave, as if suddenly overcome with shyness, and I followed Shaheen out to the hall where our horns were leaning up against the wall amid a collection of boots, shoes, and umbrellas.

Shaheen's room, like the salon, was on the second floor, and in the moment before the light was turned on I could see out into the dark branches of the trees. Then he flicked a switch, and the room was flooded with a soft illumination. If I had not been so upset, I would have been enchanted at this evidence of my friend's eccentricity, for the room was a Persian room in the old tradition. The floor was covered with a single magnificent rug from Isfahan, woven in dark, sensuous shades of red and velvety black. Apart from this, the only furnishings were a mattress which was covered with a camel's hair blanket, low bookcases, and a long, benchlike table, not more than a foot high, which held a gleaming stereo. Only a music stand and a single straight chair near the window broke the fluid, horizontal lines.

"Have to get another chair," Shaheen muttered and ducked out the door. I stood still, gazing around me at the room, which seemed to be already charged with emotion. It impressed me as a space which was at once serene and also filled with a kind of restrained passion — a room in which to enjoy the most profound peace and an arena waiting for some fierce conflict to begin. That there was going to be a row of some sort I had not the slightest doubt. That it would be our first made it no less inevitable. I wondered briefly why I was so angry and concluded that I had every right to be. The reasons I gave myself were, naturally, only the tip of the iceberg. Laleh had lit a long smoldering fuse. I had looked forward to this foreign household with a mixture of fear and fascination. It was Shaheen's home — the place where he went away from me and became an Iranian. And underlying my easy, joyous acceptance of Iran was a deep sense of its strangeness, its harsh contrasts, its secret ways. I was an outsider, intensely involved but excluded, even, I thought, scorned. Still I didn't really want to vent my rage on Shaheen. Perhaps music would weave its familiar spell and bring us together. Ensemble playing, unfortunately, does not always have this happy result. Quite the contrary.

Shaheen came back with another chair and thumped it down beside the first one. "Do you really need to warm up?" he asked before I had said anything or played a note. "After all, you were playing just a few hours ago."

"I don't care," I said. "It doesn't matter. What do you want to play?"

Shaheen opened a book of duets on the stand, and I saw that any hope of music soothing our savage breasts should

114

be abandoned. It was a collection of technical etudes written in the form of duets by some sadistic horn teacher who must have thought it more fun to watch two students suffer than one. Or perhaps he had enjoyed playing them with his pupils in order to show off his own prowess. A familiar situation.

Shaheen pointed to the first page. "This should be taken in two," he said, "but we'll do it in four to start with."

"Thanks," I said. "That's kind of you."

"It's marked presto," he pointed out.

"Why so it is," I said bitchily. "Whatever does that mean, I wonder?"

Shaheen put down his horn and looked at me with obvious exasperation. "Jill, dear girl. Do you want to play or don't you? Maybe we're wasting each other's time."

"Let's play," I said, "and take it as presto as you want. I'll scramble along behind."

The beat he gave was not, in fact, very fast, but nothing could have helped me at that point. For one thing, I was horribly aware of the whole wretched family just down the hall and around a corner. I could imagine a startled lull in the conversation followed by derisive laughter. Not that any of them would know anything about horn playing, I thought, as I made one mistake after another and finally became irretrievably lost, but they must all have heard Shaheen practicing. They would think him totally besotted to play with such an incompetent. Well, let them. "Take it from A," I said grimly, and we tried again with similar results. "Shaheen," I said, making a last-ditch effort to be reasonable, "I am really having a hard time tonight. I think it's the thought of all those people who can hear us. Maybe we should give it up after all. I'll try to be more collected next time."

"You must be more disciplined," he said. "Don't worry about what other people think. They don't know anything."

115

"You're damned right they don't know anything," I cried. "And neither do you. How do you think I feel making a fool of myself when nobody in there liked me in the first place?"

"You're imagining things and being very silly," he said. "Everybody liked you and was enormously kind."

"How would you know? You dragged me once around the room and left me stranded with your little sister who, by the way, was extremely nice to me, and just as well too. Your mother looked at me as if I were something washed up on the beach, and your beautiful big sister insulted me."

"That's crazy, Jill. They were both perfectly polite, and I thought my mother went out of her way to be friendly."

"That just shows how little you know about female behavior," I muttered. I was putting my horn away, bending over the case so he couldn't see the telltale shine in my eyes.

"I am very sorry that you found my family so disagreeable," Shaheen said stiffly. "I'll go call a radio taxi for you."

I had thought all along that it would be ridiculous for him to drive me home at this hour and had intended to take a radio cab in spite of the very considerable cost. Now it seemed like the ultimate insult. "Don't think of it," I said. "I'll get an orange cab on Pahlavi."

"Girl, are you out of your mind?" he shouted, and I had to look up. This time he saw the gleam of tears, and, to my shame, one even rolled down my cheek. He looked at me for a long moment, and when he spoke again, some of the anger had gone out of his voice. "And suppose you do manage to get an orange cab on Pahlavi without being propositioned by every man in South Tehran, and you persuade the driver to go all the way to Tajrish, do you then plan to stand outside the bazaar in the dark and try to find another one to take you to Vallenjak, or do you think the first cab you find will take you all the way home to Mummy and Daddy?"

116

"It might," I said stubbornly.

"And you also might have to take four orange cabs from this distance, as you perfectly well know," he said. "For a smart girl, you really have not thought this thing through. Now come on. I'll call a radio cab, and I'll pay for it so you won't have anything more to grouse about."

"You will not!" I shouted, and another tear rolled down the other cheek. Shaheen grinned ferociously and left the room, presumably to telephone. I knew, of course, that I was being totally irrational. The fact that in daylight hours I had perfected the art of taking orange taxis, which carried many fares at once and had to be stopped by shouting your destination from the edge of the *jube*, did not mean that it was a trick I should try at night and from such a remote starting point. Shaheen was right that I would probably have to take three or four cabs to get home from here, and while I had also become accomplished at repelling the mostly harmless advances of Iranian males, the whole experience would be very traumatic. A blond, seventeen-year-old girl standing on the street at night was liable to serious misinterpretation.

Shaheen came back. "*Panj daghighe,*" he said. Five minutes. We went for my coat, both of us surely hoping that the traditional "five minutes" of the taxi company would not stretch, as it often did, to fifteen or fifty. This time the driver must have been nearby because by the time we had walked through the garden (where the cold fountain still played and the red rose still blew in the dark wind), we could hear the impatient beep of the taxi's horn.

I let Shaheen hand me into the cab in silence. I even let him tell the driver where I was going and give him a wad of rials. I couldn't think of anything to say, but I rolled down the window anyway, and he came back and peered in. "Goodbye, Shaheen," I said. "I'm really sorry."

117

For a moment he gazed in at me smiling slightly. Then he reached through the window, and his fingers brushed my hair in a light but unmistakable caress. In a second he was gone, back through the rickety gate of his house; the driver clashed his gears, and we roared off around the corner toward Avenue Pahlavi.

I sat huddled in the back seat. The driver, faced with a long, dull trip, tried several conversational gambits. *"Farsi nist,"* I said, hoping that this horrible example of pidgin Persian would convince him that I really didn't speak the language. Apparently it did, for he mumbled something uncomplimentary and fell silent.

The rush hour was past, and there was little traffic. We headed north on the long avenue, one of the few in Tehran that went on and on without changing its name, all the way from the snowy circle of the Tajrish Bazaar to the railway station south of the Bazaar Bozorg. The shah's avenue, I thought. He could go almost from his door at Sa'atabad, straight through the heart of his city like an arrow to the station on its southern edge without ever leaving the street that bore his name. Assuming, that is, that he wanted to travel by car and train. More likely he would fly in a helicopter or in his private plane. I pictured him at the controls staring ahead with his lean, unsmiling face, his long-fingered, Persian hands hovering over the knobs and dials; and I felt stirring in my mind something quite different from the disapproval of the liberal foreigner — something much more like the hatred which radiated from Shaheen and his sisters and his friends. They were finished with this wolfish monarch in the sky, and whether they were charming like Shaheen and Shams or hostile like Laleh, their anger was the force that drove their lives. Where would it all end, and where would I be when it ended? For a moment I felt lost in a kind of no-man's-land between their stormy lives and my more tranquil one. Then I felt again that brief caress. Pitying? Apologetic? No, not at all. It was the touch of a friend, an equal, and a lover. Even if he never touched me again, I would be sure of that. I stopped shivering in my corner and straightened up, feeling a great rush of warmth and joy. "*Agha*," I said to the driver, "in truth I am able to speak a little of your language. I was tired when we began our journey."

He flashed me a happy smile, relieved to know that he was not going to die of boredom after all. So through the long drive we talked, while the dark streets fled by, the street lamps dim and yellow under the bare branches of the trees, until we came to the icy slopes of Shemiran.

"Your address, what is it?" he asked, having forgotten Shaheen's instructions in the pleasure of conversation.,

"Pahlavi, Zaferanieh, Asef, Djalal, Jilá number four," I said, which is the way you have to give your address in Tehran, where so many of the smaller streets have the same names. And soon, slipping and slithering, cursing and shouting directions, we attained our goal.

"Did my friend give you enough money?" I asked, knowing well what the answer would be.

"Perhaps not quite enough for the length of the journey and the ice and the snow and . . ."

"Please accept a little more," I said, reaching in my pocket and cutting short this litany of tribulations before it could become any longer. "*Khoda hafez*. I hope you have a good trip back."

"*Insh'allah, khoda hafez, khanoum*," he said, and drove away.

I came into my familiar home with the feeling of having returned from an immense journey and found that it was only eight o'clock. My mother was setting the table for dinner while Ali chopped the salad into minuscule fragments in the kitchen. Dad was reading at the end of the couch. James lay on his stomach at the exact center of the rug with a drawing pad. I regarded this scene with deep affection, thinking how nice the nuclear American family really was.

"Oh good, you're home," my mother said. "We were just wondering whether to eat, but I didn't think you had gone for dinner."

"No. Help! What an awful idea," I said.

"How was it?" my father asked. "I'll bet you're stuffed with tea and Iranian goodies."

"Terrible," I said. "Really. You know how the Fahouris seem to have this constant stream of visitors? Yes, well Shaheen's house is the same. I had to meet all his relatives and speak Farsi and eat things drenched in rose water, and then Shaheen's room where we went to play was just down the hall, so I had visions of the whole tea party listening to all my mistakes. The more I thought about it, the worse I played. Honestly, I hope never to have to do that again. Shaheen will just have to come here."

They were laughing at my tale of woe, and I could see that it *was* funny — all but my quarrel with Shaheen, and this I kept to myself.

"You'll probably go back often," Dad said. "It won't be so bad the second time. Once you know what to expect, you can handle it."

Ali came in to announce dinner, but first he had to satisfy his curiosity about where I had been. "Missus Jill, you where?" he demanded, glaring at me, arms akimbo.

"*Manzel-e-Agha* Rohani," I said defiantly.

"Ha," Ali said. "Many rugs, no?"

"Many, many, many rugs," I said, "and now, let's have dinner, Ali."

"Okay, I am dinner," he said and went back to the kitchen while the rest of us assembled at the table.

I went to bed early that night and had one of those dreams well known to horn players in which one suddenly finds oneself in the first chair of the Boston Symphony Orchestra and unable to produce a note. This is almost as bad as being chased by something and unable to scream. In the end, Shaheen came in and said kindly, "You'll be playing fourth today, Jill," so I moved down to the end of a row of about twenty horns with a feeling of immense relief. I don't know exactly what problems this solved for my unconscious, but I was then able to get a good night's sleep.

Chapter 16

*My father had been right when he pre-*dicted that I would visit the Rohani house many times and even grow accustomed to the rituals of the ongoing tea party. I also became quite friendly with most of the family, with the notable exception of Shaheen's mother, who continued to regard me with faint but unmistakable distaste. The early part of January, however, was occupied by a political storm which left everyone shaken and with little interest in the social aspects of life.

President Carter's visit to the shah, during which he expressed approval of all the policies of the Pahlavi government, might almost have been designed to encourage revolution in Iran. It was followed about a week later by an extraordinary article in the *Etelaat,* one of Tehran's two leading newspapers. This article, which many believed had been written by the king himself, attacked the Ayatollah Khomeini, calling him a medieval reactionary, slandering his character, and holding him responsible, despite his long exile in Iraq, for a wide spectrum of national woes. It might seem from the vantage point of history that any denunciation of Khomeini was probably well deserved. At the time, however, the vast majority of the Iranian people saw him as a heroic and much abused leader, working in the background until the time came for him to save his country. Even our sophisticated and irreligious friends held this view. The great Ayatollah seemed in those days to be the distillation of all that was pure and brave enough to bring down the king.

It is hard to see what inspired the government to its vicious and ill-timed attack, but what was immediately clear was that it was a terrible mistake. Not only the mullahs but all the factions of Iranian society that had grievances against the shah were now united in their sense of outrage.

In Qom, the religious center of Iran, there was a sit-in during which twelve demands were read. They were demands which any citizen of a Western democracy would approve — demands for freedom of speech and assembly, for elections, and for a return to constitutional government. Following the sit-in, four thousand students marched in the streets of Qom, where they were fired upon by the police and scores were killed or wounded. Even more horrifying was the report that blood donations had been forbidden by the police, so many more died after they had reached the hospital. This was the first of the major riots which were to be repeated throughout the year, culminating in the total revolution that destroyed the Shah of Iran.

For me it was a traumatic time but also an exciting one. All of the Iranian students at school were in an uproar and it was clear that many of the rich, lazy young people who had been indifferent or even vaguely pro-monarchy before were turned around both by the tastelessness of the newspaper letter and by the appalling events in Qom.

Shaheen, of course, went about in a state of white-hot rage and frustration. His black stubble emphasized the pallor of his face, and the light of battle was in his eyes. Unfortunately, at least from his point of view, there wasn't any battle to fight except on the verbal level. Tehran buzzed with protest, but there were no confrontations. He and his fellow enthusiasts had to content themselves with impassioned meetings which went on far into the night and greatly impaired my social life. This is not to say that my sympathies were elsewhere. The revolutionary fervor was catching, and this time the action was sufficiently far from home that I could ride the wave of excitement without being scared out of my wits at the same time. Though I saw little of Shaheen and was not invited to any meetings, he spoke openly to me about his feelings and his hopes for the coming revolution. I felt for a few days as if I was a privileged witness at a great moment in history.

Soon, however, there began one of those periods of strange and ominous calm which characterized the early months of 1978 in Iran. Following the precepts of the Koran, the Moslem population began a forty-day mourning period for those who had died in Qom. They would take no more action until late February when a memorial service in Tabriz would end in an even more violent explosion. Shaheen and his friends fumed and plotted, but since no one can stay in a state of high emotion when nothing is happening, they, too, eventually calmed down, and life resumed its normal course.

Like the period around Christmas, this midwinter lull in public events was one of extraordinary joy in the private sector. Shaheen and I went everywhere together. We played duets at both our houses, and after I got to know some of the regulars in the Rohani salon, I was able to take a more carefree attitude toward our invisible audience.

More snow fell on Shemiran. We threw snowballs, went sledding, fell off the sled, and tussled like puppies in the drifts that filled the *jube*. This horseplay was agreeable, even though it did lead me to further speculations about the American girl who had preceded me in Shaheen's affections. What charms had she possessed that I must lack? If I was being treated with some kind of elaborate respect, I could live without it. If he really did not find me attractive, which by now seemed unlikely even to me, the problem was more serious. No matter; it was all a delight. And Shaheen was looking marvelous with his dense, short beard trimmed as he had promised like that of some Elizabethan courtier. My parents, prejudiced as always, maintained that I, too, had undergone a change for the better; and I had to admit that all this happiness and winter weather had done my looks no harm.

Chapter 17

*I don't know what made Shaheen sud-*denly decide that I should meet his father, nor why it took him so long to get around to it. At any rate, one day after school he said with deceptive lightness, "I know what we'll do today. We'll go to the bazaar and sip a cup of tea with the old man."

I let my mouth drop open and took a quick inventory of my clothes. They could have been worse, but they also could have been a lot better.

"And don't worry about your clothes," Shaheen went on, casting an appreciative glance at the deep vee of my sweater. "My father will like that neckline as much as I do."

"He's not strict about this sort of thing?" I asked dubiously.

"Good Lord, Jill, don't confuse my father with Ali," Shaheen said.

I laughed. "Don't worry. I'm not that mixed up about Iranian society. Poor Ali. He spends half the time trying not to look at me when I'm wearing something like this that I never even thought about before."

"Ali has a real problem," Shaheen said. "He's probably living a life of torment there in the same house with you. You have no idea of the Moslem prohibitions he struggles with — Don't touch a woman until you're married. Don't look. Don't even think a lustful thought. Naturally," he added with a ferocious grin, "nothing could be better designed to encourage lust than a long list of forbidden delights."

"I should think you have escaped most of this," I said, "your father being, as you say, quite a different sort from Ali."

"But the restraints are everywhere," he said. "They're in the very air you breathe."

"I know," I said. "I don't know whether I could live with it all the time — the feeling that one is being sinful just walking around in normal clothes, to say nothing of giving a friend of the opposite sex a little squeeze from time to time. I think it must be bad for people."

"Bad doesn't even begin to describe it. Boys like Ali are savage with frustration and also with guilt, because, of course, they break the rules anyway in spite of their fear of God and the mullahs. I'll bet you didn't even know that Tehran had a red-light district." I shook my head, trying to look less fascinated and more sophisticated than I felt, and Shaheen went on with obvious relish. "Absolutely. It's quite large and very well organized according to specialty. But the largest part is devoted to the very young and very desperate — five minutes for a couple of *tomans* — that sort of thing."

"So then I suppose they feel physically better but mentally worse," I said, repressing my desire to ask him how he knew so much about it.

"Most of them feel meaner than hell most of the time,"

Shaheen said. "And then they turn their anger against the women, who have problems of their own — sitting around the house gnawing at the edges of their chadors, or so I have always imagined." He paused for a moment, frowning, and then continued in a more optimistic voice. "Of course, they turn against society too, and that has its advantages when one is planning a revolution. All this pent-up sexual rage is hard to beat when you want to get something done, like removing a king or tearing down a few palaces."

"Shaheen," I said, "that's horrifying."

"Horrifying but true," he said cheerfully. "And now behold the Bazaar Bozorg and its usual horrendous parking problem. Did you know you can drive a car through the bazaar on a Friday?"

I shook my head. "It must be weird."

"Weird and still a bit hair-raising. There continue to be little old men lurking around every corner. Anyway, what one can do on Friday doesn't solve our problem today."

Finally we found a semilegal parking place not more than a half mile from one entrance to the bazaar and set out to wend our way through the dense crowds in the narrow passageways. The rug bazaar is itself immense but quieter than other parts of the Bazaar Bozorg, perhaps because of the relative costliness of its merchandise. You can buy a small and undistinguished carpet here for as little as fifty dollars, but you can't buy anything for fifty cents. This naturally thins out the hordes. We padded along between two rows of cavernous shops. Some were open to the passageway and had their sumptuous wares spread out before them. Others were closed and secret-looking. Here and there we saw groups of people gathered around rugs which lay in pools of sunlight that came through the glass panes in the roof of the bazaar.

The Rohani establishment had glass doors set in ornate iron-work and a sign in Farsi and English picked out in gold leaf. The English portion of the sign said "Finest Oriental Rug from All the World."

The interior of the shop was dim, but artfully placed spot-lights shone on the masterpieces that hung around the walls, making them glow as if with a light of their own. I knew by now enough about Persian carpets to realize that here I was in the presence of greatness — greatness and an immense amount of money, I couldn't help thinking. The rugs on the walls were antiques, many of them woven of silk, others of the finest, most closely knotted wool. A boy was engaged in spreading a huge golden Turkoman for a disdainful-looking American couple, while across from them stood what could only be the carpet king himself, watching the whole thing with a slight, cynical smile.

"How much is this one?" the woman asked.

"Three thousand five hundred dollars," said Agha Rohani promptly. "But I will offer you a discount. "Three thousand. It is worth twice that amount in New York."

The woman turned to her husband and spoke in high-school French. "C'est trop," she said. "Offres lui moins."

Shaheen's father continued to regard them blandly across the rug while I squirmed with amusement and embarrassment for my compatriots. French was hardly a secret language in the bazaar. Many of the older merchants spoke it better than English. The suggestion that an international businessman like Rohani might not understand such infantile phrases made these Americans seem unbearably provincial.

At this point, however, he glanced in our direction, and his face lit up with quite a different smile, one which was warm and genuine and entirely for us. "Will you excuse me?" he said to his customers. "I see that I have guests. Please tell the boy to show you anything else you may be interested in while I make them comfortable."

We joined him, skirting the Turkoman and the now baffled-looking couple. He greeted me by taking my hand in both of his and gazing into my face with lively dark eyes. Shorter and heavier-set than his son, he had the same grace of manner and the added charm of European courtliness. I wondered how anyone with a penny to spare could resist buying the first carpet that Agha Rohani might suggest. "I know you are Shaheen's good friend, Jill," said this delightful man. "I am so happy to meet you at last."

"I am happy to meet you, too," I said.

"Come into my office," he continued. "We will have tea, of course. What else? And perhaps," he went on in Farsi, "we will get a chance to talk a little while these bright people make up their minds."

I laughed, pleased that he would joke with me in Farsi and that I could show I understood. His office was a tiny cubicle in one corner of the shop. It was walled with glass so that he could keep an eye on his customers and his assistants, another of whom had now appeared to hover over the American couple. There was barely room for an overflowing desk and the three straight chairs on which we perched. Almost immediately a boy appeared with tea. Shaheen, who had been silent until now, said, "I hope we're not going to cost you a sale out there."

"Fear not," his father said. "If they go, they will return. They have heard, you see, that I am the only honest rug dealer in Tehran, and while they don't believe that I am honest, they will be afraid to try anyone else. And, of course,

130

a carpet they must have. They can't go home without one."

"Maybe you can sell them the white elephant of Kurdistan," Shaheen said.

Rohani laughed. "You'll see. Someday I will find the right person for that monster, but I think not today."

"This rug," Shaheen said, turning to me, "is the biggest damn thing you ever saw, and it really is mostly white — unusual to say the least — and beautifully woven. Unfortunately, it is as ugly as it is impractical, and even the master con man of the bazaar here doesn't seem able to unload it."

"How did you get it in the first place?" I asked, surprised that this wily merchant should have anything he didn't want.

"Took it from a friend for a debt," he explained. "Here in the bazaar we do each other favors and hope to turn a profit at the same time. Perhaps I made a mistake with the white elephant, but I think my patience will be rewarded in the end. A rich foreign couple — German, perhaps — will come in the door. We will talk a little, and I will know the truth: These people have a passion for white. They can foresee the problems — the cleaning bills, the exclusion of children and pets and even friends. All this will only make them desire it more ardently. Psychology. I could teach a course in psychology. To do well in the carpet business you have only to be a good mind reader and have enough stock to cover a wide range of human peculiarities. In the end there is a carpet for every customer and a customer for every carpet."

"That's what Shaheen told me when he was looking for something to go with our terrible furniture," I said. "And by the way, we are enjoying the rug you found for us very much. It is far and away the most beautiful thing we have ever had."

Shaheen's father gave a dismissive, wave of the hand.

131

"Please do enjoy it," he said, "and don't worry about it. No obligation, you know. I am happy to have been of service. If you do end up wanting to buy it, however, I will make you a genuinely good price," and he shot a wicked smile in the direction of the sales floor.

"Thank you," I said. "I know you will, and I hope we can, but we seem to be out of money most of the time in spite of getting more of it from the oil company than we ever had before. Maybe when they pay us off at the end. We're supposed to get all kinds of lovely extras at that point."

"Don't count on it," he said. "I don't want to alarm you, but don't count on it, and you should tell your father to start asking for his airline tickets right now. They are always nice to have tucked away somewhere when you work for an Iranian company. As for your chronic money shortage, that's nothing new. Everyone in Iran has it to one degree or another. This economy is a disaster area, and His Imperial Majesty there," he jabbed a finger at a point just above our heads, "has seen to it that the people in the middle pay for it."

I turned my head and saw the stern visage of the shah staring down at me from the official photograph that had its place in every Iranian business or shop and in nearly every home (although some hid it away in dark hallways or even, in one case I heard of, in the bathroom). This one was rather small, given the prestige of the establishment, and one side was overlapped by an exquisite prayer rug.

"But there seem to be lots of rich foreigners," I ventured, "and, as you say, they all want to buy carpets."

"Rich foreigners," he said scornfully, cutting the air with his hand in a sharp, negative gesture. "The rich foreigners who matter to us never come near Tehran. They stay in London and Munich and New York and wallow in Persian car-

132

pets. And that's good!" He smiled at the thought of all that trade, then scowled again. The bazaar used to *be* the economic life of Iran. Now we sit here and fume, waiting for the next royal inspector to come and stick his long nose into our business."

"You're preaching to an already confirmed antimonarchist, Father," Shaheen said mildly.

"Is that so?" Rohani regarded me with even greater interest. "Ah, but she is probably a young radical like you. Shaheen wants to give the country to the people," he explained to me, and it was clear from the way he said "people" what he thought of their worthiness to run a country. He was certainly no democrat, I reflected; but I liked him enormously just the same.

Shaheen, however, was looking uncomfortable. He put his teacup down in a welter of telegrams and invoices and got up. "Let me show Jill some of our nicer things," he said. "Your fish still seem to be on the line out there. Perhaps you can now proceed to haul them in."

"Anything to avoid a good political brawl," his father said jovially and took my hand once more as I stood up to go. "We must talk again soon. I am pleased to see that my son has better taste in women than in politics."

This time I did blush to the roots of my hair. I was beginning to see why Shaheen had put off this visit. "Thank you," I mumbled. "I hope we will. Thank you so much, Agha Rohani."

The three of us went out into the shop, and the merchant rejoined his customers with a suave apology while Shaheen led me around the walls, pointing out his favorite treasures. He seemed to know a great deal about each one, and as he explained the traditional designs and the intricate craft of rug weaving, I could see that, though he might care little for his father's business, he had the most profound respect for its beautiful products. When we reached the door, I turned back and saw Agha Rohani standing in his perfect English suit in the middle of a field of red and gold. With one fine hand he was pointing out some feature of the rug to the American couple, who were watching him with glazed eyes like rabbits before a cobra.

Chapter 18

It was during this winter interlude that I got my biggest dose of Persian culture. By this time I was ready for it, and I knew several people who were eager to educate me. Shaheen, of course, was my most enthusiastic mentor.

The first concentrated lesson came, somewhat improbably, on my birthday. I had neglected to tell Shaheen of this momentous event until the day before. Even then I might not have mentioned it if he hadn't suggested that we go out the following night. I had to tell him then that my family would be expecting me for a birthday dinner. To my surprise, he looked completely crushed.

"You might have given me a little warning," he said.

"I'm sorry, Shaheen," I said. "I just thought — well, I just didn't think. Stupid of me."

"You'll pay for it when you have to eat a whole box of rosewater sweets, which is about all I'll be able to find between now and tomorrow."

"It's the thought that counts," I said comfortingly, and was rewarded with a baleful glare.

Naturally it had crossed my mind that Shaheen might give

135

me a birthday present, and I really should have given him time to comb the bazaar. What he came up with was, in its way, far better than some more conventional gift. It was lying on my seat in the car when we came out of school the next day.

"Well, there you are," he said as he unlocked the doors. "There's your box of *shiriniye golab.*"

It was, in fact, a beautiful copy of the *Shah-nama,* the great Persian book of kings written by the poet Ferdowsi and illustrated by the sixteenth-century artists who have made Persian miniatures famous throughout the world. The reproductions were magnificent, and the text was in Farsi. I contemplated it with a mixture of delight and misgiving.

"Shaheen, it's beautiful," I said. "I've always wanted a *Shah-nama,* and this one is splendid. Thank you."

"But you're wondering how you're going to read it," he said, grinning wickedly as he started up the car.

"I suppose that's not the most important thing," I said dubiously.

"On the contrary. Ferdowsi was one of the greatest poets of all time. But don't worry. You will learn to read it. Let it serve as an inspiration in your studies."

I peered at the beautiful but enigmatic calligraphy. Farsi is a much less difficult language for Westerners than Arabic, but it is written in Arabic script from right to left with most of the vowels left to the imagination of the reader. This makes reading it quite a different proposition from speaking it. By now I had learned enough to make out a word here and a word there, but they still didn't add up to a poem, and I secretly doubted that they ever would.

The darkest part of the winter was now over, so there was plenty of light for me to study my book as we drove home from school. The miniatures seemed almost to spring out at

136

me from the pages, so fresh and vivid were the colors. They teemed with brightly dressed human figures, animals, birds, flowers, and strange beasts. "Who are these different-colored creatures with human bodies and animal heads and tails?" I asked.

"*Divs*, of course," Shaheen said.

"How nice and how appropriate," I said. "We get two of our words for devil from Farsi — *shaitan* and *div*."

"Mmmm. Divs are older, I should think, older and more pagan. They were very powerful, but you can see that in this picture they are getting the worst of it. Not only is the infamous black div being killed by the young prince; two others are being savaged by lions and a leopard."

"And there is a brave man in the foreground," I said, "who seems to be pulling a brown one by the tail."

"Foolish fellow," Shaheen said. "I doubt that that was wise, and the blue div and the white div are going to get away to fight another day. The prince, by the way, is Hushang, who is avenging the death of his father, Siyamak, at the hands of the black div. That's his grandfather, Shah Gayumarth, watching the battle from horseback."

"Help, slow down," I said. "I've never heard of these people. Should I have?"

"Never heard of Gayumarth?" Shaheen asked in mock horror. "He was merely the first shah of Iran. That's like saying you've never heard of George Washington."

"Don't be silly, Shaheen. You know perfectly well there's no comparison. What about Cyrus? I thought he was the first, or almost the first."

"Oh, Gayumarth was way before Cyrus," he said, and I continued to have the feeling that I was being gently teased. "Gayumarth was king at the beginning of the world, before the coming of evil. Then Ahriman, the first div, came along and all our troubles began. The black div was the son of Ahriman, and he killed Siyamak, the son of Gayumarth."

"The light is beginning to dawn," I said. "You're talking mythology, not history."

"That's the nice thing about Persian history," Shaheen said. "It is so hard to tell where fact leaves off and myth begins."

We had come to one of the customary impasses in Tehran traffic, and our little car sat in a sea of honking vehicles and milling Iranians of all descriptions — businessmen in European suits, construction workers from the desert with ragged turbans and baggy pants, girls in short skirts and high heels, housewives muffled in black chadors. Shaheen reached over and turned back the pages of the *Shah-nama* to a picture of such magical beauty it took my breath away.

"Gayumarth and his court before evil came to the world," he said.

The king was enthroned on a stylized mountaintop from which sprang the gnarled branches of flowering trees. Below him his court stood in a circle around a little meadow that brimmed with flowers and animals. More animals could be seen among rock formations of oriental intricacy on either side. The colors were more gentle than in the other miniatures but had great depth and richness, the dark green of the field and the bronze sky accentuating the delicate violet shades which surrounded the king and his white-robed courtiers.

"This one is very famous," Shaheen said. "See how many animals you can find among the rocks, and in some places the rocks themselves have animal forms or even the profiles of human faces."

I studied the picture again. It was like those children's puzzles, the ones that say, see how many whatsits you can find in the branches of the tree. While we worked our way north, I turned the pages of the book slowly, and Shaheen told me the stories that every Iranian child knew by heart. Here was someone with the improbable name of Gushtasp slaying a wonderful black dragon; there little white-haired Prince Zal sitting naked on a blue and purple crag looked over by a motherly *simurgh*, the Iranian version of the phoenix. In still another a wicked man named Zahhak was being chained to the wall of a cavern on the summit of Mount Damavand "so that his brain might chafe and his agony endure," as Shaheen quoted with relish. Below this grisly scene was a cheerful, picniclike gathering presided over by the young hero Faridun, looking very dapper in his blue tunic and yellow tights. I glanced up and saw the real Mount Damavand shining in the east beyond the dunes of Abbass Abad.

"Shaheen," I said dreamily, "when are we going to climb Damavand?"

He looked thoughtful. "Maybe July," he said. "We have to wait until full summer and get into good condition with other climbs. It won't be long now before we can start up the lower valleys again."

"Really?" I cast a dubious look at the snowy foothills.

"Really. Spring is almost here, you know. By late February we'll be able to go to Pas Qaleh again or Haft Hoz or up through Vallenjak. There will still be lots of snow, but most of it will have melted off the lower trails."

"A short winter, but a merry one," I said. "When does it get really warm and lovely?"

"By No Ruz in late March. When you see the what-do-you-call-thems, the *banafsh* everywhere, you will know that spring and the New Year have arrived together."

I consulted the battered green dictionary that never left

139

my side, and after a brief struggle with the two missing 'a's, found *banafsh*. "Pansies," I said delightedly. "Do you have pansies?"

"We are positively awash in pansies," Shaheen said.

I leaned back with a contented sigh, imagining Shemiran in bloom and the mountain valleys running with water from the melting snows.

As we turned up the hill from Avenue Pahlavi, I went back to my book. Shaheen stopped the car in front of the house and leaned over to see the picture I was studying. "That's old Ferdowsi himself," he said, reaching across the page to point out a bearded figure dressed in red and green. His hand brushed across mine where it lay on the open page, hesitated, and came to rest. I raised my head slowly, feeling the warmth and firmness of his touch. He was smiling, his black eyes full of gaiety and challenge looking into mine. "What was I saying?" he said after a long moment. "Was it important?"

"About Ferdowsi," I said in a dazed voice and turned my hand over so our fingers laced.

"Enough of Ferdowsi," Shaheen said. "We'll finish your education another time."

At this promising moment, the front door slammed and Ali bustled forth with a broom and started to sweep the steps. "Damn that boy!" Shaheen cried, letting go of my hand and flinging open the car door.

"This is the first time he has ever been known to sweep out here," I said furiously as I gathered up my things.

"Your guardian angel," Shaheen said, as he opened the door on my side. "We should get him wings, a red robe, and a turban and set him to hovering over you like the ones in the miniatures."

"I would shoot him down," I said. "Odious boy. Why can't my parents bring themselves to get rid of him?"

"Because, like you, they are softhearted or softheaded depending on your point of view. Now go have a staggering feast, and I'll see you tomorrow."

"It's already been a perfect birthday," I said.

He gave a quick smile and touched me lightly on the cheek. Then he was back in the car and roaring off up the street in reverse.

I stalked into the house without greeting Ali, who contented himself with giving me a black look. Enraged though I was in a local and temporary way, I was not, on the whole, at all displeased with life.

Chapter 19

*Although I had largely overcome my feel-*ing of panic at the thought of the entire Rohani family listening to our horn playing, I continued to regard Shaheen's room with mixed emotions. I was happy to be there, but I felt a bit as if I had stepped from the streets of Tehran into a chamber in the Arabian Nights. Sumptuous, serene, above all sensual — it always made a slight shiver go up my spine.

On one visit to the Rohani house, I found a beautiful, shiny black cat curled in the exact center of Shaheen's bed. I went down on my knees at the edge of the mattress, and she opened a pair of eyes as blue as sapphires, yawned, and uttered a complicated, questioning sound. "Why Shaheen," I said. "She's at least half Siamese. Did you know that?"

"What makes you think so?" he asked, sinking down beside his pet and running his fingers gently down her spine.

"First the blue eyes, of course, and then the voice. That's a dead giveaway. Other cats meow; Siamese cats talk."

"Yes, constantly," he said, laughing delightedly.

"And the half-breeds are often black," I added.

"Such a fund of miscellaneous information," he said. "She has a name now, by the the way. Shams named her."

"She would, of course," I said. "No little girl is going to live with a cat for very long without giving it a name. Least of all Shams. What was the outcome?"

"She is called 'Jamal,' " Shaheen answered gravely.

"Perfect," I said. "How wonderful names are in foreign languages. I suppose *'jamal'* sounds as trite to you as 'beauty' does to me. Still . . ." I ran my hand over the shiny, black fur and quoted, "'She walks in beauty like the night of cloudless climes and starry skies . . .' "

"Go on, please," Shaheen said.

" 'And all that's best in dark and light meets in her aspect and her eyes,' " I continued. "That's all I know. Sorry."

He was looking at me dreamily. "You must learn more poetry. You're constantly whetting my appetite and then quitting."

"You must read more English poetry," I answered severely. "You can't expect me to fill the gaping holes in your education from memory."

"It wouldn't be the same," he said. We gazed at each other fondly across the body of the luxuriously stretching feline, and Shams came in without knocking.

This brings me to the other point about Shaheen's room. It was a space made for the most delicious intimacy, which was constantly being invaded without the slightest ceremony. As time went on, I found this aspect of Iranian life increasingly hard to take. We were often alone, but we never felt alone except sometimes in the mountains. Because of the coming of winter, it had been some time since we had been in the mountains. In the car, of course, we had total privacy for conversation, but our every move was observed with avid interest from the sidewalk and, even more, from other cars which were tangled up in the same traffic jams with us. In the house, Shaheen's family popped in and out, not with any apparent desire to snoop, but simply out of natural gregariousness.

None of the above was any excuse for the maddening physical restraint of my beloved. Since I am neither a practiced nor an aggressive female, all I could do was wait and ache as seductively as I could manage. Meanwhile the emotional charge built up like a thunderstorm on a hot night, and I longed for it to break as the dry earth longs for an expected rain.

This time it was Shams who came bounding into our sieve-like sanctuary and shattered yet another promising moment. She seemed delighted to see me and greeted me like an old friend.

"Hi, Jill," she cried in English. "You have meet Jamal. Is she not beautiful?"

"Dear sister, please save your English until it is better than Jill's Farsi," Shaheen said with some asperity.

"Don't be mean," I said. "She needs to practice, and I think her English is charming."

"There's a time and a place for the charm of little sisters," Shaheen grumbled, but by this time Shams had ensconced herself firmly between us and almost on top of the cat.

Jamal, for her part, abandoned her role of great lady in repose and rolled over on her back with a seductive growl. Would it were so easy, I thought, as we all fell to tickling her furry tummy.

We chattered and played with the cat for a while longer. Then Shaheen told Shams that we had to practice, and she left, promising to return promptly if we paused too long for breath.

When we had set ourselves up to play, I saw that Shaheen had put the second horn part to Beethoven's "Egmont" Overture in front of me. Mr. Perenyi had decided, with more

144

bravado than good sense, that this beautiful transcription would make a striking finale to the spring band concert, and so it would if we could possibly learn to play it. Unfortunately, from my point of view, the best parts were for first and second horn. It seemed unkind of Shaheen to tempt me with this coveted part, and I said so.

"Learn it anyway," he said. "Who knows what the future may unfold?"

"Shaheen," I said severely, "if Helmut suffers another terrible misfortune, no one is going to believe it was an accident."

"Violence was the furthest thing from my mind," he said, "but I am determined to play this piece with you. Look at that duet, just for example. That one there. Can't you hear us? Helmut wouldn't make any mistakes, but that's not enough. When you and I hit those chords, the audience is going to be shot right through the heart."

I laughed and picked up my horn. "All right then, let's learn it, but I promise you, if I have to sit back and listen to someone else play this part, I shall expire right there in front of everybody covered with green spots from head to foot."

"Trust me," Shaheen said, and we began to work on Egmont. After a while, I stopped worrying about who was going to play what in the concert, which was still several months away, and threw myself into the joy of playing Beethoven with Shaheen.

Chapter 20

The religion of the Shia Moslem is dark and intense, focused on mourning and on martyrdom. On the days of Tasua and Ashura during the holy month of Moharram, groups of men go through the streets beating themselves with chains, bewailing the death of Hossein, thirteen centuries ago. So after forty days, the names of the dead in Qum became a battle cry in the mosques and courtyards of Tabriz. Soon the whole city flared into a new and more aggressive form of violence. As in Qum, religion was the torch that lit the fire — but Tabriz is a more political city, in which hatred of the central government has always flourished. For every voice that cried out to Allah, another shouted, "Down with the shah! Give us elections and free speech!"

For three days that began with religious services on Friday, the Tabrizi fought the police in the streets, turned over cars, burned banks; and the police fought back. They were later criticized by the shah and censured by Parliament for using guns against unarmed people, but that did not lessen the effect of the riots. By then it was too late, and these

146

moderate gestures were interpreted as another sign that the government was feeble and unfit.

The events in Tabriz frightened our family and had a nearly disastrous effect on my still fragile love affair. We heard the first news on the radio Friday night, and afterward I could hardly sleep. To make matters worse the next day was a school holiday, so I had far too much time to worry. At about ten o'clock I tried to call Shaheen. Laleh answered the phone, which was an improvement over one of the grandmothers, but what she told me did nothing to relieve my anxieties. "He's gone to a meeting," she said. "I was just leaving to join them."

"What kind of meeting?" I asked stupidly. I knew the answer perfectly well, but I wanted to keep Laleh on the phone in the hope that she would let fall some crumb of information. Her voice reflected a heroic effort to be patient.

"You must realize, Jill, that students are meeting all over Tehran to discuss these new outrages. We are trying to decide whether to go to Tabriz or to stay here and organize our forces for a possible uprising in Tehran."

"Much better to stay here," I said. "It's a long way to Tabriz in buses or whatever you were thinking of. By the time you got there, it would probably all be over and nothing left to do but come home again. Demoralizing, I should think."

"What makes you think it will all be over?" Laleh asked. She sounded as if she thought I had some kind of hotline to the riot police.

"How would I know?" I said. "It didn't last long in Qum."

"Maybe this time is different. Maybe this is really the beginning."

"Then you can stay here to get your heads broken," I said.

"Just be patient and trouble will find you. That's an old family saying."

"Well, I must go," she said abruptly, "but don't worry. I am sure you and your family are in no immediate danger."

"That's not the point," I shouted. "I want to talk to Shaheen. At least tell him I called."

"I'm sure he will call you when he has time," she said and hung up, leaving me angry as well as fearful.

The rest of the day was miserable. Shaheen did not call; the family tried without success to cheer me up; and grim reports continued to flow from the radio. I tried to practice but felt strangely short of breath and uncoordinated. Toward evening I walked to the bakery. The snow was gone now, and crocuses were beginning to bloom in grassy patches along the *jube*. Briefly the sound of running water and the sight of mountains standing quiet against the darkening sky soothed my nerves. But the evening was as bad as the day had been. I went to bed exhausted and slept with troubled dreams.

To my surprise and temporary relief, Shaheen came to school on Sunday. I saw him at lunch hour standing by the kiosk deep in conversation with some Iranian students. Watching his swift, fierce gestures and the way his black eyes blazed in his pale face, I sensed how far he had withdrawn from me into the world of revolution. But still I set myself to wait, planted firmly in his line of sight. About two minutes before class time he finally broke away and came over to my side.

"Hi," I said. "You look as if you'd been up all night."

"I have," he said. "I wouldn't have come to school except that I needed to see some people here."

"Some people but obviously not me," I said. I hadn't

meant to let my feelings show so much, but the sight of his stern, preoccupied face brought all my misery to a head, and the words came tumbling out. "I left a message for you to call me yesterday morning," I went on. "You could at least have done that."

"I'm really sorry, Jill," he said. "This is a very hectic time for us."

Again that feeling of exclusion — of being someone who was reserved for the less serious moments in life. I was becoming angry, which was an improvement on my pitiful mode. "I see you decided not to go to Tabriz," I said. "Good thinking. That was a harebrained idea if I ever heard one."

Shaheen didn't rise to the bait. Probably I wasn't even worth quarreling with. "We decided our place was here in case the fighting spread to Tehran," he said.

"That's what I told Laleh," I said. "There's ever so good a chance of getting shot right here if you'll just wait around a bit and not go charging off into the blue. My God, you might be out in the desert somewhere in a broken-down bus and miss all the excitement."

At this point the class bell prevented me from lashing myself into an even greater lather. To do him credit, Shaheen now looked truly distressed. "I've got to talk to you," he said desperately, "but not today after school. I must go to another meeting. Please try to understand." And he dashed off without giving me a chance to say that I would.

I trudged drearily to my American history class and sat for forty-five minutes not hearing a word, repeating over and over to myself: Yes, I'll try to understand. Of course I will. But exhorting myself to understand failed to make it happen. My head had that numb, stuffed-up feeling you get with a bad cold; and it was impossible to imagine how any useful thought could form in that mass of dead or dying neurons.

Shaheen did not come to band rehearsal. Probably he had decided to cut the rest of his classes. I had to play first horn — a lost opportunity since I missed one note in three. At last the ghastly day was over, and I was on the school bus with my nose buried firmly in a book as a deterrent to conversation. It was not that I never rode the bus in the afternoon any more. I did so at least once a week and sometimes without anyone making a catty remark, but on this particular day I didn't feel up to verbal fencing of any kind. Unfortunately, it is always on such occasions that one's friends feel most witty.

"Poor Jill. Has to ride with the plebes." This was Georgia, my least favorite person from band, and I saw with horror that she was about to sit down next to me. I nodded with a small, chilly smile, not looking up from my book. "Have a fight with Shaheen?" she continued cheerfully, plunking herself down in the seat.

"Georgia," I said, "please tell me why it is impossible for me to ride the school bus just like anyone else without a court case being made of it."

"Shaheen is busy playing at being a revolutionary," said Margot Hamidzadeh from across the aisle. Margot was half Iranian and one of the few staunch monarchists I knew.

"Why? What's happened?" Georgia asked.

"Have you heard of Tabriz?" I said wearily. "Have you the slightest inkling of what is going on up there?"

"Oh that," Georgia said. "That'll all blow over. My dad says there's nothing to worry about."

"Of course it will," Margot said. "The riots have already been contained and the Communist agitators have been arrested."

"I like your style," I said. "You sound like a SAVAK news release."

"I don't understand," Georgia complained. "What has all this got to do with Jill and Shaheen?"

"What indeed?" I said. "Exactly nothing except that Shaheen is busy, and I am busy. I have a huge paper due tomorrow, so it would be really nice to be left *alone.*"

I returned to my book and, rather to my surprise, was left in peace. Georgia turned her back on me to talk to Margot. If they were talking about me, I neither heard over the general racket of the bus nor cared. I turned the pages and stared at the print. It was true. I did have a paper to do. The very thought made my bones ache and my head swim. Perhaps I was going to be sick, maybe very sick. I would lie in bed and let the world struggle on without me. Perhaps Shaheen would visit me and hold my hand. It all came back to the same thing.

Needless to say, nothing of the sort occurred in the days that followed. My occasional desire to play the invalid is always frustrated by my robust health, and even my depressions seldom last for long or cause much anxiety among those near and dear. Still, it was not a cheerful time. By Tuesday the rioting, rather than being "contained," had simply spent itself. It did not spread to Tehran. About a dozen people appeared to have been killed, a small number perhaps, but even one person shot by the police is one too many. The country settled sullenly into another forty days of mourning.

After Sunday Shaheen returned to band rehearsals, playing with his usual offhand brilliance, being civil to everyone but really friendly to no one. He seemed tired and uncommunicative. We talked of the music and little else, but from time to time I turned my head to find his dark eyes gazing at me with an intense seriousness I was at a loss to under-

151

stand. Finally on Wednesday before we left the band room he said, "I'll take you home today, Jill. Wait for me in the usual place."

I looked up from my horn case on the floor. "That would be nice," I said, "if you're sure it's not . . ." I stopped abruptly. How could I have even thought a sarcastic remark at a time like this? "That will be nice," I repeated lamely.

He favored me with a faint, weary smile. "No, it will not be too much trouble," he said. "Any more than it's ever been."

I met him under the old plane tree that shaded the grass between the main building and the outer wall of the school and followed him silently to the familiar little car.

Shaheen gave his usual attention to starting the engine, which coughed and spluttered once before it caught. "Have to have the car overhauled," he said.

"Too bad," I said. "How long will it take? Getting from here to your house on public transportation could be a drag."

"Not that bad. Anyway, I can borrow Laleh's car. She doesn't take it to work — doesn't want to arrive in her god-forsaken village looking like a great lady."

"I think that's very sound," I said, and he nodded. Normally this would have been a perfectly good conversation opener, leading into all kinds of fascinating topics. Today it seemed like a dead end. We both fell silent and stared out through the windshield, on which a few large raindrops were beginning to fall.

"It will be pouring in Shemiran," Shaheen said gloomily.

"And snowing in the mountains," I added. "Are you sure spring is just around the corner?"

"It's supposed to be," he said.

"Why are you so depressed?" I asked bluntly. "I've never seen you like this."

152

He shrugged. "I don't know. Anticlimax. Letdown. We all got too excited. You know how it is."

"Not really," I said. "After all, I have never had the dubious privilege of belonging to a revolutionary cadre or whatever you call it."

"Neither had I before," Shaheen said, "and I must say that the group aspect of it is rather trying. Meetings, meetings, meetings. Words, words, words. I am not a good follower."

"Then you must become a leader," I said.

He looked at me strangely. "I was almost chosen to lead our group," he said, "which would have been an honor considering my age."

"What happened?" I asked with a sinking feeling.

"I believe I was judged to be politically unreliable, in some sense not quite sound," he said.

"Guilt by association," I said. "How horribly unfair!"

"It doesn't matter," he answered, but without conviction.

I didn't know what to say. I could see that the gulf between us was going to widen if I didn't do something, but for the moment, it seemed hopeless even to try, and we struggled on through the increasingly wet traffic in silence.

Finally I said, "Shaheen, I just want you to know one thing. I really do believe in the same things you believe in, and whatever happens, I am always on your side."

"That's good to know," he said, without looking at me.

"But you don't believe it," I said forlornly, "or it doesn't much help."

"You always have something negative to say," he answered.

"I know, and I'm truly sorry. But you have to understand how ambivalent I am about violence and how frightened for your safety."

"Then that is an important difference, isn't it?" he said. "Because I am not at all ambivalent about violence nor the least bit concerned about my personal safety."

"I said I was on your side no matter what," I said, "and I meant it. That should mean something to you."

"It does," he said, "and I appreciate it, Jill, but I don't think all of this is getting us very far at the moment. Let's talk about something else."

Easier said than done. I couldn't think of another topic that wasn't totally trivial and irrelevant. Up ahead of us two cars came together with the familiar sound of tortured fenders, and the creeping traffic stopped while the drivers leapt from their vehicles in order to scream at each other face to face. Shaheen wrenched the wheel over, drove up on the sidewalk, narrowly missing several pedestrians, then swerved back into the street ahead of the accident.

"Wretched Tehrani," he said surprisingly. "They ought to put a driving school on every corner."

His voice was thick with fury, but I guessed that it had little to do with the routine irritations of driving in Tehran, with which he was usually very patient.

"The trick would be getting people to go to driving school," I said. It was something to talk about, and that's what we did the rest of the way home.

This ride set the mood for all the subsequent rides over the next two weeks, and during most of this time the skies continued to rain, drizzle, or simply frown upon the city, so you can imagine just how cheery the last part of February was. Shaheen went to more student meetings. When there weren't any meetings, he drove me home, and we talked nervously of general topics in which both of us had lost interest. I almost wished that he would leave off for a while and let me ride the school bus; but that would have meant

154

total defeat. So long as we were seeing each other, there was a chance for improvement. I did what I could to act normally and made a heroic effort to look as attractive as possible, even though clothes and hair styles were lower than usual on my list of interests. I really couldn't fathom what was going on, but later it seemed obvious that Shaheen had decided to break with me but couldn't bring himself to do it — a far happier conclusion than I was able to come to at the time.

Chapter 21

Then suddenly on a Wednesday after-
noon, almost two weeks after the fighting in Tabriz, the sun
came out. It shone on Tehran — on the streaked concrete
walls, the muddy lanes, the naked trees — and it shone into
the darkest corners of our unhappiness, transforming everything. If the weather had changed a week earlier, it would
not have made the slightest difference in how we felt, but
when it came, we were ready for it. The joy we both took in
life had been driven underground, submerged in misery and
strife. And there it had grown like some marvelous crystal in
the dark, needing only one ray of sunlight to shine forth
again.

We were driving north on the expressway when the clouds
began to part, and the sun struck through onto the drenched,
brown dunes. The change was swift in the freshening wind.
Before we had come to Avenue Pahlavi, the grubby rain
clouds had become glorious mounds of whipped cream top-
ping the white peaks of the Alborz, and the hills swam in a
sea of light.

I looked at Shaheen and saw my smile reflected on his
face. "*Farda be kuh miravim,*" he said, speaking Farsi to me

for the first time in weeks. "Tomorrow we will go to the mountains."

"I'll pack a lunch," I said joyfully.

"Don't make too much. We can buy fruit and cheese at the foot of the trail in Darrakeh."

"Darrakeh?" I said. "That means we can go to Haft Hoz again."

He laughed. "You sound as if that was another word for heaven."

"I'm not sure it isn't," I said, leaning back and closing my eyes, remembering the seven green pools shining among the hot, lizard-haunted rocks, the walnut trees, the jagged valley leading up and up. "The storm has rolled away," I added softly.

Shaheen gave me a slight, enigmatic smile. "*Shayad*," he said, using that most Iranian of Farsi words with its overtones of doubt, hope, and cynicism, meaning so much more than just "perhaps."

"*Rasti*," I answered with conviction. *Truly*. And he reached out and touched my hand briefly, almost shyly, before turning the car up the hill on Zaferanieh.

At noon the next day we parked the car as high as we could, then went on foot to the top of the village of Darrakeh. The gorge was full of water rushing down from the mountains, and when we reached the bridge, we stopped to stare down at what had been in the fall a junk heap with a miserly trickle winding among the tin cans. Now it was a formidable cataract which had either covered or washed away the refuse.

"Where did it all go?" I wondered.

"Down to Tehran, I imagine," Shaheen said.

On the other side of the bridge in the small store nestled at the foot of the mountain trail, we bought fruit and goat

157

cheese and two floppy rounds of lavash from a boy who had just arrived with a great folded pile of it clipped to the back of his bicycle. These items joined the bottle of white Iranian wine in Shaheen's pack, and we were ready to climb.

The trail goes almost straight up from behind the store, then levels out and follows a more leisurely course above the stream. To our right we could look down among plane trees on the village women washing their clothes in the cold, swift water. To our left the naked rocks climbed in savage formations against the white wall of the mountains.

After the first scramble we were able to walk abreast, and I turned smiling to Shaheen and held out my hand. It seemed an entirely natural thing to do, and he grasped it firmly as if we had been walking this way for half our lives. Feeling those long fingers laced with mine, climbing together in the thin, bright air, I felt an enormous surge of joy and hope.

"We must do this more often," Shaheen said, and I nodded, speechless with happiness.

At Haft Hoz the trail comes down to meet the stream, and there are the seven pools for which the place is named. The water has carved them into rock of a beautiful, icy green. They climb the valley in a twisting chain, each linked to the next by a low waterfall. There was still snow under the overhanging rocks, but I knew how inviting these pools could look after a hot climb.

"We'll come back here and swim," Shaheen said, "though even in August you freeze your ass off. I promise you."

I laughed. "This is a risk I may not be willing to take."

"It feels terrific," he said. "The trick is to scramble up through all the pools before you turn blue and your toes drop off. Yes, really. You'll see how nice it is. Oh look, a what-do-you-call-it bush."

He slid down the riverbank, pulling me by the hand, and there, against the snow-streaked rocks, was the most magnificent pussy willow I had ever seen. "It's a pussy willow," I said, "or it's the father and mother of all pussy willows. I've never seen one so huge."

"It's perfectly normal for these hills," he said, "but what a funny name. I don't know what they are called in Farsi."

"*Bid-e-gorbe?*" I tried out dubiously. "See. We call these catkins." I reached out a finger and stroked one of the furry buds. It was as large as the end of a man's finger, an opalescent, silvery gray shading to pink. The long branches were full, the catkins bursting with soft, mysterious life. Shaheen, too, reached out to touch — first the bud and then my face. A moment later he was kissing me — first just a soft brush of lips, then hard and long. I closed my eyes and felt his mouth and the strength of his hands. It all felt just as I had always thought it would, only ten times better.

At last Shaheen let me go. "My God I love you," he said. "What a ridiculous amount of time we have wasted." And he kissed me again.

Our picnic bag had slid to the ground, and after a while we both noticed it lying there with the neck of the wine bottle sticking out. "Shall we chill the wine?" I said, "or just guzzle it as is?"

"Let's chill it," Shaheen said. "It won't take long, and we can easily occupy the time." He took the bottle to the nearest pool and wedged it between the rocks in the clear, running water. The sun was warm now on the bank. There was a patch of vividly green grass where Shaheen spread his denim jacket for us to sit. It wasn't very big, but then, it didn't need to be. Under the jacket he was wearing a white polo shirt of some incredibly soft material against which I leaned my head, feeling the warmth of the sun, the hand that

159

stroked my hair, the other arm that was tight around me.

When the wine was cool, Shaheen pulled the cork and filled two plastic cups. I watched his sure, graceful movements with intense pleasure, as if I were seeing them for the first time. We toasted each other gravely, wordlessly. There seemed no longer any need for words, but after a pause he said, "We mustn't let anything come between us again."

"Hush," I said. "Nothing ever will."

He regarded me thoughtfully. Then he said, "I was well on my way to kissing you when that miserable affair blew up."

"True," I said, smiling, "but still, you had all winter. What took you so long?"

"It was too important," he said. "I wasn't going to play any games with you, Jill. And besides, you are not exactly a forward young lady yourself."

"All I need is a little encouragement."

"That I can provide," he said, and went on to show me what he meant.

We drank the wine slowly and before it was gone, discovered that we were ravenously hungry, so we ate the bread and cheese and most of the fruit. No meal ever tasted better, except perhaps the one at Pas Qaleh.

"I fell in love with you at Pas Qaleh," I said, "I mean really, fatally, as opposed to just being mad about you. It seems so long ago."

"I know," he said. "That's where it happened to me too."

I don't know how long we sat together beside the mountain stream, but finally the shadow of the cliff fell across our place, bringing with it the sharp chill which the desert air can have when the sun has gone. We got to our feet rather stiffly, and Shaheen said, "Well, it was a short youth but a merry one."

"You'll soon be warm," I said. "Put on your jacket. It's damp but better than nothing."

"Positively clammy," he said, shivering as he pulled it on. "Never mind. Let's wander on a bit up where it's still sunny, and I will dry out."

I put my arm around him under the jacket to protect him from the cold cloth, and we meandered up the trail, climbing out of the shadow into the warm air of the afternoon, up toward the gleaming mountain pass. In places the trail was slippery with mud or melting snow, and we clung together laughing.

Just as we were about to turn back, a man on a donkey appeared on the trail above us, and we waited for him to pass, standing circumspectly with our arms at our sides. The donkey was slung with empty Coke cases, and I wondered to what remote place his cargo had been delivered. The man frowned as he came toward us but stopped, and we exchanged the traditional greetings. Then he said something to Shaheen, and I caught the words "foreign woman."

"Be quiet, Babá," Shaheen said. "The woman is my sister."

For a long moment the man studied us, comparing my insignificant nose with Shaheen's impressive beak, my straight blond hair with his wavy black. "*Shayad*," he said at last. "*Insh'allah*," and, giving his beast a kick, he moved past us and down the trail.

"Was that amusing?" I said when he had gone, "or not so very?"

Shaheen put his arm around me again. "A little of both," he said, "but don't let it bother you. We shall have to get used to that sort of thing and practice agonizing amounts of restraint most of the time in Tehran."

"What a bore," I said, "but it's not a new idea."

"It just means one hell of a lot of mountain climbing," he said, "to make up for lost time, as it were." And we gave our attention to another lengthy kiss.

"If only we could store them up to parcel out through the week," I said finally.

"What an idea," Shaheen said. "Freeze-dried passion, or possibly canned."

"We will patent it and become rich," I elaborated. We were both giddy with relief at the release of long-pent-up emotions as we slithered and slid our way back to Darrakeh, stopping by the pool to cut an armload of branches from the pussy willow bush.

We climbed into the car in the narrow village street under the enthralled gaze of several urchins and a very old man. Shaheen started the engine, lit a cigarette, and gave it to me, our fingers brushing in the old, familiar gesture of intimacy. We smiled at each other secretly, contentedly, leaving unspoken the thought that now these gentle signals were a promise rather than an end in themselves. A great sense of peace had descended on us, and we drove down through the market square of Darrakeh and out into the hills again in silence. As we passed Evin Prison Shaheen said softly, "Don't look," and I nodded, thinking, Now we are reading each other's minds.

We stopped in front of my house and sat there for a minute holding hands while all of Shemiran seemed to be watching us. A brief shadow crossed Shaheen's face. "Well," he said, "this is the way it's going to be. Are you free tomorrow?"

"As a bird," I said. "Don't you want to come in for a minute?"

He shook his head. "I don't want to see anyone but you just now," he said. "I'll call you in the morning. Good night, my love."

162

"Good night, Shaheen," I said, and slipped from the car. Anyone seeing this lack of formal courtesies might have thought that we had quarreled.

The sky today is a gentle, luminous gray, stretching over land and sea like a benediction. It is at once vast and comforting, like a soft blanket drawn over the world by a kindly god. The gulls are crying far out on the black rocks, and I think, why should these watery voices call me back to white mountains burning in a desert sun?

I walk by the sea with the spray in my face, enveloped in dreams as in the fine mist off the face of the sea. At first I tried to forget those days, but now I know the deep virtue of remembrance. I will not let that gold be washed from my mind by the currents of time, but will keep it always stored against future poverty.

"Nothing is lost," I say to the waves. "Nothing is ever really lost."

Chapter 22

March is the month of the New Year for Iranians, and No Ruz, which falls on the spring equinox, is their only joyous holiday. It is not a Moslem holiday but a pagan celebration going back to Zoroaster's religion of light and fire. It is a time of splendid feasts and delightful, non-religious rituals, of colored eggs and bowls of goldfish and bonfires in the streets. The whole thing lasts for thirteen days and ends with a picnic in the country. We contented ourselves with buying the traditional bowl of sprouted wheat and watching the delicate shoots grow into a cloud of green. On the day of the picnic we were to throw the whole thing into a running stream, disposing thus of a year's bad luck. Though the Iranians seemed preoccupied with the evils of the past and with hope for the future, I found it hard to think of anything in the past year with which I would willingly part.

The whole of March that year was a time of constantly unfolding joy. At night I seemed not so much to sleep as to live in a world of dreams which vanished in an instant with the light, leaving behind only a sense of some great happiness — the memory of a state of bliss lingering like the fragment of a haunting melody. Each day I went to my window to see how far the strange, curled leaves of the fig tree had opened in the night, then barefoot across the cool, stone floors to the front of the house to see the mountains bathed in early sun, their white flanks now streaked with brown. Behind the mud-brick walls and in the steep lanes of Shemiran, one by one according to their kind, the flowering trees came into bloom. Then came the promised *banafsh*, the heralds of the new year. Vacant lots were suddenly transformed into Persian carpets of pansy flats in all their multitudinous shades of purple, rose, yellow, white.

Through all this splendor I walked with Shaheen, and each day was a celebration. We begrudged our time in school, but now the late afternoons were light, and our weekends were planned to the minute, as was the long holiday which would begin on the twenty-first.

On the second Friday in March we drove out of Tehran, far west on the highway, then off on a gravel road that wound among the hills. We entered a world of vast and daunting loneliness, the desert realm where mystics read prophecies in a million stars, and the word of God is branded into their souls by the midday sun. The road was rough; even in this wet season a plume of dust rose behind the car; but when we stopped, it was beside a stream that ran full and clear under a low stone bridge. The willows along its bank were cascades of golden green against the brown slope of the hill, and a few steps more found us ankle deep in violets. Shaheen looked up at the top of the hill, which was as flat as if it had been smoothed off with a gigantic spatula. "This is what we are looking for," he said. "Come, girl. Now you must climb."

"I didn't know we were looking for anything," I said, taking his hand as we started up the long slope. "How could you find anything out here — any particular thing, I mean?"

"You'll see," he said, "or at least I hope you will. It's been a long time since I was here."

We came out at last at the top of the hill and stood gazing around under the immense sky, the fabled Persian sky one never sees any more in Tehran, depth upon depth of fathomless blue. I saw then that we stood among ruins. Fragments of broken wall stretched away from our feet, and in one place someone had started to dig, disclosing intricate stonework going down into the earth. "This is a *tepé*," Shaheen said. "There was once a palace here or a city wall. I don't know what it was or how old it is — three or four thousand years at a guess."

"My God," I said, with an American's awe for anything more than a few hundred years old. "Why isn't it crawling with archeologists?"

He shrugged. "These places are all over Iran. Some of them are being worked, of course, but there's no way we can do them all." Swiftly he bent and picked up something from the ground. It was the fragment of a pot, earth-colored, scarred by time but showing still one graceful curve. Shaheen ran a finger gently over the shard. "This is our history, he said. "Four thousand years. Four hundred and forty-six kings, and Mohammed Reza Pahlavi the last. It makes me wonder if we are standing at some momentous crossroads, or if all our brave deeds are only a puff of wind to stir the sand. This is why I come here every now and then."

I put my arm around him, feeling suddenly cold in the March sun, chilled by the sense of history, as if the wind were blowing through us into the future out of this unimaginable past. For a long time we stood like that among the sparse ruins of a forgotten race, looking out over the soft dunes to the mountains in the north. Then Shaheen dug me in the ribs.

"Come on," he said. "We can't spend the whole day wallowing in enormous thoughts. There's a picnic waiting in the car. Let's go do something about it." So we charged off the edge of the mysterious *tepé* and down the hill, slipping and sliding in the scree, laughing, breathless, ordinary.

We ate our lunch under a willow on a bed of white and purple violets. Then we got down to the other serious business of the day. While we were thus engaged, a shepherd and his dog wandered by on the far bank of the stream. Shaheen disentangled his face from my hair and glared at the man's retreating back. "You wouldn't think this country could be so damn populated," he said. "We'll have our next picnic on the Dasht-e-Kavir."

"What's that?" I mumbled into his shirt.

"The great salt desert," he replied.

"It sounds unattractive."

"It is," he said. "That's what makes it such a good place to be alone."

"We'll take a camel," I said, "and it will gaze at us with those huge, dark eyes all camels seem to have."

"And spit on us from time to time."

"Oh stop. You're no fun."

The shepherd seemed to have settled down for a nap on the green hillside across from us. Shaheen gave an exasperated laugh and pulled a small book from his pack.

"Literature time?" I asked, referring to the fact that he had made me keep my promise to read English poetry to him. Now it would seem that I was about to get some back.

"It isn't quite what I had in mind," he said. "Poetry is a poor substitute for the real thing, but maybe you can help me with this one. I find your older poets difficult."

I looked over his shoulder and saw that he had the poems of Andrew Marvell. "All right," I said. "You're a glutton for punishment, but go ahead."

Shaheen opened the book at a well-worn place, gave me a smile of angelic sweetness, and began:

> *"Had we but world enough, and time,*
> *This coyness, Lady, were no crime."*

I listened as he read, beautifully and with all too perfect comprehension, the famous lines, and the blush I hadn't felt in weeks crept slowly upwards from my toes.

> *"The grave's a fine and private place,*
> *But none, I think, do there embrace."*

He paused and looked up at me.

"Shaheen," I said severely, "*shaitan*. You know perfectly well what every word of that poem means."

"Do I?" he said. "I was hoping you would explain it to me."

I shook my head, smiling. "Not a chance, honey."

"Oh well, then I shall have to explain it to you. It means . . ."

"I know what it means, Shaheen," I said.

He brushed my cheek with his fingers in the gentle, tentative gesture I knew so well. "You are going to sleep with me, aren't you, Jill?" he said.

"Yes!" I said suddenly, fiercely, surprising myself, for it was certainly a question I had asked myself before, coming first to one conclusion, then another. "But wait a little, Shaheen," I added, surprising myself again.

He studied me gravely. "You know the rest of the poem?" he asked, and when I didn't speak, went on:

> *"But at my back I always hear*
> *Time's wingèd chariot hurrying near;*
> *And yonder all before us lie*
> *Deserts of vast eternity."*

For a moment I stared at him, feeling the chill of those deserts in my heart. And I think if I had known then how swiftly the future was rushing upon us, I would have lain down with him there under the green fronds of the willow tree and let the shepherd wake or sleep as the case might be. I took his hands in mine and said, "I know and I promise. Soon. But where and when? Our lives are so complicated."

"Leave the details to me," he cried, leaping to his feet.

I was infected by his happiness but in the car driving home, I saw that Shaheen was again pensive, almost sad. "What is it?" I asked. "Didn't we have a terrific day?"

"Yes," he said, "fantastic. But I was just thinking, you know, that it is almost forty days since Tabriz."

I had not forgotten that horrible time, but I had put it in the back of my mind and, like many other people, both foreign and Iranian, I had begun to ignore the inexorable progress of the revolution. I supposed Shaheen had done the same. Certainly our lives had not left him much time for political meetings, unless these took place in the darkest hours of the night. They did, as a matter of fact, and he was far better informed than I had dreamed.

"There will be heavy demonstrations again," he went on when I did not respond, "this time in Tehran."

"Back into the nightmare," I said in a low voice.

"Yes," he said, "I know what you mean. Now I know. But try not to think of it that way. Try to think of it as something we must go through before things get better — as winter before spring."

"But this is spring," I cried, looking out at the flowering hills, feeling sudden tears burn my eyes.

Shaheen took my hand. "This time will be different in every way," he said. "In some ways it will be worse because it is here, and you are here. Don't think I haven't worried about all this. But it can't divide us the way it did before. You know that, don't you?"

I nodded, blinking back the tears, gathering my strength. "There's another thing, Shaheen," I said. "This is all very fine and spiritually satisfying, but in a practical sense what it means is that I am not going to leave you — physically, that is."

He looked at me sharply. "I'm not sure I know what you're saying."

"It's really very simple," I said. "All I am saying is that I am going to stay with you — I, Jill Alexander, American girl revolutionary — in the flesh as opposed to some more mystical way. So don't think you are going to go out and get your head bashed, leaving me at home to pine and sigh. That is what you were thinking, I presume?"

"Impossible," Shaheen said.

"Impossible, hell," I said. "I'll even put on the disgusting chador if I have to, with a big safety pin under my chin, so just put that in your calculations."

"Well, we'll see," Shaheen said pacifically, and he patted

my hand which he had released in order to deal with the driving complications around the bazaar.

"And don't pat my hand," I said, at which he laughed and made a more serious grab for me, an attempt which was frustrated by a sudden call for both hands on the steering wheel.

"When is all this fun going to start?" I asked as lightly as I could, when we had pulled up in front of the house.

"Oh, not for several days — maybe not at all," Shaheen said. "You never know with these things."

"I am not reassured," I said. "But let's do something fabulous tomorrow."

"We will," he promised. "I'll call you, love."

I found my mother and Ali arguing fiercely in front of the glass door that opened onto the tiny courtyard in the center of our house. Ali was making pleading gestures towards the square of green grass on which I now saw, strutting proudly to and fro, a truly magnificent orange rooster.

My mother stamped her foot. "He brought this home from the country," she cried, "and now he wants to murder it in the bathtub, and then I suppose he wants me to cook it. Well, I won't, and I won't have blood all over the tub either. So, *na*, Ali. *Na, na, nakher. Mifamid?*"

"I understand," Ali said in Farsi, with unwonted patience. "I will cook. I will clean the bath. It is a good rooster and will be delicious."

"It's so beautiful," I said. "Why not let it live a little, Ali?"

He looked at me as if I had lost my mind. Not for a pet had he lugged the creature all the way from his village in a suitcase. "*Mohem nist,*" he said. "Never mind. I will kill it in the driveway."

"You will not," my mother said.

"Ali," I said, seeing that the battle for the rooster's life was already lost, "Shemiran is full of empty lots. Just take it away from the house like a good fellow."

Ali made a gesture of despair at the sensibilities of foreigners and advanced upon the rooster while my mother buried her face in her hands. We had, in fact, a vacant lot right next to the house, and there, when I went out for one last look at the mountains in the dusk, I came upon the remains of Ali's sacrifice lying in a pool of blackened blood. Slowly I picked up one bright feather from the sad little pile. It seemed to blaze in the waning light and then grow dull, as if death had overtaken it in my hand.

Whether the dinner, prepared for once without my mother's expert touch, was good, I really couldn't say. I fed myself in my room on barbari and cheese.

Chapter 23

On the eve of Chahar Shambe, which is the fourth day of No Ruz, we stayed late at school to see a play. When we came out through the gate we saw bonfires flaring up the whole length of the street, throwing wild shadows on the battered walls as figures ran and leapt in the lurid glare. A cross section of the whole world seemed to be cavorting there — students of every nationality and Tehrani of every age, shape, and size. There were fires to suit all the members of this varied throng, from tiny ones for children and for the women encumbered with their long chadors, to great, roaring blazes for the most daring adolescents. Once in a while, if one threatened to die away, a dark figure would dart forth with a can of gasoline, and up it would shoot again, while the crowd laughed and cheered.

I looked at Shaheen and saw his bearded face alight with the fires in the street and with a fierce, interior joy. "Come on, Jill," he cried. "Let's jump the fires and burn up all the bad luck from last year."

I regarded the savage scene with fascination and misgiving. Jumping has never been one of my prime accomplishments, and I am afraid of fire. "How many must I jump?" I asked. "Won't one be enough?"

"One will do the trick," Shaheen said, "but you'd be missing half the fun."

"You have the fun," I said. "I'm going to wait until there is one my size — just before one of those fiends pours gas all over it. Go on. I'll watch and admire."

"And you with such great long legs," Shaheen said. "All right. Hold on a minute. I'll be back to make sure you don't shirk the whole thing."

I watched him run to the end of the block and held my breath as he returned, leaping with a dancer's grace — sometimes, it seemed, right through the highest flames. He came back to me radiant and out of breath.

"Beautiful," I said. "But you smell scorched. Are you sure you're not smoldering somewhere?"

"Absolutely not," he said, after a quick glance down at jeans and sneakers. "Now it's your turn."

"How about that one?" I said, pointing to a neglected heap of glowing coals.

"That won't do a thing for you. Come, we'll jump a modest blaze together for double luck." He grabbed my hand, and before I knew it, I was up and over quite a respectable little fire and down on the other side, laughing and hugging Shaheen.

Open affection seemed to be all right on this wild night of festivity. For a few hours the barriers were down, and a pagan spirit reigned, uniting people who were worlds apart, loosening the bonds of a strict society.

We drove away slowly through the old city, pausing to look down alleys where more fires burned, more shadows darted in the flickering light. The business district was as cold and dull as always, and Avenue Pahlavi retained its bourgeois dignity. But up in the little lanes of Shemiran, where the poor still lived, we glimpsed again the bright, celebratory flames.

Chapter 24

The first Tehran demonstration came a day earlier than Shaheen expected, and we were caught in the middle of it. I often ask myself what we thought we were doing on Shah Reza across the street from Tehran University at a time like this. It was certainly not the place for anyone who wanted to keep out of trouble, since the university was already well known as the focus for the city's political discontent. Shaheen, of course, did not want to keep out of trouble, but he had made it quite clear that he meant to ditch me in some safe place at the smallest hint of violence. At any rate, there we were, prowling through one of the many bookstores in that area, when we heard the sirens of the riot police. Shaheen turned pale and went to the window. I became aware of the shopkeeper's eyes on me. "You should go home," he said. "There will be trouble now." I shook my head and followed Shaheen.

We had both seen crowds of students milling around on the lawn behind the iron gates of the university, a sight too common in those days to be noteworthy. Now masses of them were pouring through the gate into the street, and we could hear the police loudspeakers telling them to go back to their classes. Shaheen was quivering like a racehorse at the starting line, but he turned to me with an air of gentle reasonableness.

"I see someone I know, Jill," he said. "Just stay here a minute while I try to find out what's going on. Then we'll split."

He should have known better. I produced my most docile smile until his back was turned, and was out the door on his trail one second later. In jeans and sneakers I was more than a match for him. When he dived into the crowd, which was now blocking the heavy traffic on Shah Reza, I was close enough to grab his shirttail any time I wanted to. This was just as well; I might be brave or foolhardy, but I had no desire to be alone in this mob of strangers.

To my relief I saw that it was a mixed crowd of young men and women and that while some of the girls had their heads covered with big kerchiefs, many were bareheaded, and there was not a chador in sight. Although placards bearing the picture of Ayatollah Khomeini were bobbing above the heads of the demonstrators, I doubted that religion was their only motivation. These were young radicals like Shaheen. Probably they had been listening to political speeches on the lawn when someone decided that there were too many of them and called the police. There were also signs saying "Death to the shah," "Avenge the Martyrs of Tabriz," and one which read, "Down with American Imperialists," which did nothing to quiet my pounding heart.

"Well, here you are, you brilliant girl, right where you always wanted to be," I said to myself. Except I really hadn't wanted to be in this mob scene. I had only wanted to stick with Shaheen, and this appeared to be no easy matter. Realizing that he couldn't very well send me back now, I made a dive for his belt before the crowd closed around him.

He turned with a startled look, and for a moment I thought he hadn't recognized me. Then his eyes widened. "All right then, come on," he said, and grabbed my hand.

It was hard to tell what was going on. Ahead loomed the tops of the police vans with their loudspeakers barking orders which were totally ignored. The iron fence across the front of the university and the stone pillars were draped with students. Some of them were shouting bulletins to the crowd below, but my Farsi was not equal to the confusion, and I caught only a word here and there. Something shaped like a tin can flew through the air and landed behind us. A roar of anger went up, and a moment later I felt my eyes sting. "Tear gas. The bastards," Shaheen shouted. Then, lowering his head, he charged forward in the direction of the police. My eyes hurt, but it was not too bad. "They can't put us down with puny stuff like that," I thought and dashed the tears off my face with one grimy hand, keeping a tight grip on Shaheen with the other.

Suddenly the ranks in front of us broke, and we could see the police standing with their backs to their vans. They had gas masks on, and their guns seemed to be pointing straight into our faces. It was the most terrifying thing I have ever seen. Another canister flew, but someone caught it and threw it back. At the same time the police raised their guns and fired into the air — or at least some of them fired into the air. When the terrible noise of the shots had died away, we could hear someone screaming over the roar of the crowd. The faces of the students around me were contorted with fury. Shaheen dragged me to one side and up against the back of a newspaper kiosk. The top of the little structure was already thick with demonstrators, but almost before I knew what was happening, he had scrambled onto the shoulders of another man and then to the top of the kiosk. He was shouting something to the crowd. I clung to one of the shaking wooden supports, able to think only that he was a perfect target up there. "Strike now! Now!" I heard him cry, and the crowd surged forward, engulfing police and vans in one furious rush. There were more shots, more screams. I felt my hand being pulled and realized Shaheen was down and dragging me again toward the center of the mêlée.

I don't know how much time passed or what happened during the horrible confusion that followed, but my fear evaporated, and I lived only to join the others in doing whatever damage could be done to the murderers in gas masks. More tear gas had been released, and our eyes were streaming, but we hardly felt the pain. Somehow we found ourselves with about twenty others pushing on one of the police vans. We heaved with an enormous collective strength, and the thing went over, narrowly missing another group that was attacking it from the other side. Someone shouted "Back! Back!" and we staggered through the gates of the university just as an explosion ripped the air and a plume of fire leapt from one of the disabled vans. "Good," Shaheen cried. "They've made some Molotov cocktails. Now we'll see some action."

"What have we been seeing?" I screamed back, amazed at my ability to joke in such circumstances.

I was rewarded by a flash of white teeth in a smoke-blackened face, but Shaheen continued to pull me back among the trees of the campus. "No point in being fried," he said. A lot of people apparently felt the same way. The crowd on the grass was almost as thick as the one in the street had been. There was another explosion, another burst of flame, and we all cheered. Now, however, we became aware of sirens which seemed to be coming from every part of the city, closer and closer, screaming their message of fear. A chill ran through me, and looking at Shaheen I saw that he, too, was afraid. "Come," he said. "We've done all we can. Let's head for the west gate and see if we can work our way back to the car. It sounds as though they're bringing in everything they've got. At least we showed the bastards they should think twice before trying to break up a peaceful assembly."

I wasn't sure we had done anything of the kind, but I was one with him in his desire to get away from the university. It was beginning to get dark by the time we gained the west gate. We could hear sirens in the next street, and we still had to walk maybe a dozen blocks farther south to find the car. At this point, I realized that I had somehow twisted my ankle, and it hurt like hell to walk. Shaheen had a cut on his forehead and streaks of blood through the dirt on his face. Had someone been throwing stones? I couldn't remember. We stumbled on, pausing only to let a shrieking squad car go by before crossing Shah Reza. The streets to the south were quiet, and the shopkeepers had pulled down their shutters. This peacefulness had a bad effect on me. I sank down on the edge of the *jube* and tried to ease my ankle into the trickle of water flowing there. Shaheen knelt beside me. "How bad is it?" he asked.

"It hurts," I admitted, "but it's just a twist. I thought maybe some cold water, but there doesn't seem to be any." Suddenly I was aware that my teeth were chattering, and that I was shaking from head to foot.

"Touch of shock," Shaheen mumbled. "Can you put any weight on it? Here, wait a minute." He took off his shirt, tore a piece off the bottom, dipped it in the tepid water of the *jube* and wound it tightly around my ankle. It felt marvelous as long as I didn't move, and I could feel the shakes subsiding a little.

"Sorry," I said. "It was such a nice shirt."

"I think it was done for anyway," he said, putting the top half of the rag back on. Then he reached out and pushed the straggling hair back out of my eyes. "You were fantastic, by the way," he said.

I shook my head. "All in a day's work, but let's do something else for kicks tomorrow."

"I hope we can," he said gravely, "but I have a feeling that this is only the beginning."

Tears stung my already reddened eyes and I lowered my head hoping to hide them. In one part of my mind I knew he was right, but it was not a fact I was prepared to face just then.

"What we need is a good hot cup of tea," Shaheen said, holding out both hands to help me to my feet, and I had to laugh at this homely banality. If standing was horrible, walking was worse, but I found I could do it, and at last we made it to the car.

There were about twenty students gathered around the fountain in the Rohani courtyard when we arrived. They stopped talking to watch our painful progress, but I was past caring about social awkwardness. Shaheen led me to a stone bench and installed me with my back to the end and my foot up. By the time this was done, a maid had appeared from the house with tea for us. It was an incongruous scene — the filthy, battered young revolutionaries, the elegant old garden, the servant gliding around with tiny teacups. A paper lantern from No Ruz illuminated the fierce, exhausted faces around me, and to the north the budding branches of the trees were outlined against a dull, red sky. It was war and peace encompassed in a few short blocks.

Now I saw Laleh standing near the fountain in jeans and a tattered, black sweatshirt. Her curly hair stood out in all directions, and her face was streaked with soot, but her stance conveyed a kind of triumphant joy. Shaheen crossed over to speak with her, and the others resumed the excited talk which had been interrupted by our entrance. I leaned back, sipping my strong, sweet tea, and felt the last tremors subside and a mild sense of euphoria take their place. I could understand little of what was said, but I did hear "*dokhtar-e-amrikai*" several times and felt their bright, black eyes flick over me. It was Laleh who put a stop to this discussion of the "American girl." She strode over to one of the men and said in a low, commanding voice, "Enough, Hossein. She is one of us."

He turned his head and stared at me for what seemed an eternity, then smiled with a flash of white teeth. "Welcome then," he said and turned back to the others.

Shaheen came and sat on the end of my bench and put his hand in a gentle, proprietary fashion on my battered ankle. I felt as if I had won the triple crown, and relaxed still further into my tea.

The talk flowed on; the fountain played; a light wind stirred the branches against the ominous sky. The others were making plans; that much I could tell, but for the time I didn't even want to know *what* plans. In spite of Laleh's accolade, I doubted that they included me, and that was exactly the way I wanted it. Tomorrow I could start to worry about Shaheen again. For the moment it was enough to be both safe and accepted.

After a while some of them rose to go. "Better wash up a bit first," Shaheen said, and I knew he was thinking of the police, who might well be on the lookout for smoke-blackened strays. So they went into the house in twos and threes, emerging many shades lighter and fading out the gate into the strangely quiet streets. I wondered what the elder Rohanis thought of all this.

Some of the group lived, I knew, in Shemiran. That bastion of wealth and privilege was also the largest breeding ground for the young, intellectual left; and I asked Shaheen if one of them couldn't take me home. "I was going to take you myself," he said.

"Don't be a loon," I said. "You would probably run straight into a *jube* on the way home. If no one is going my way, I'll call a radio cab."

"Maybe Ali Reza," he said, and I guessed, from his willingness to consider the idea, how exhausted he must be. He left me for a moment and spoke to a stocky young man who was standing near the gate, and came back nodding his head. "That's fine, then," he said, "but I didn't want to let you go so soon."

"We've had a rich, full day together," I said. "And now do you think you might find another fragment of your shirt or something to dip in the fountain so I can wash my face? My parents are going to have a stroke when they see me, but at least I can scrub off some of the soot. This will strengthen my story that I was running away the whole time."

"I'll do better than that," Shaheen said, and made off for the house. He came back with a warm washcloth. "Move over an inch, if you can," he said, and, sitting down beside me on the bench, he began, gently and methodically, to wash the dirt away. We were very close, and I thought how nice it would be to stay that way forever, with his leg pressed against my side and his long fingers doing pleasant things to my face. It couldn't last, and despite my good intentions, I dreaded parting from him to go home with a stranger. "Shaheen," I said, "don't go anywhere without me. Promise."

He stopped dabbing for a moment and smiled at me. "You're going to be slowed down for a few days, my love, but I will call you. Often. I do promise that." He bent and kissed me lightly but firmly on the mouth, then leaned back and surveyed me critically. "I think you'll do in a dim light," he said. "Please tell your parents I tried to take care of you."

"I will," I said, struggling to my feet. "Don't worry about that. Ouch! Damn."

Shaheen helped me out the gate and into Ali Reza's small but expensive car. "I wish you boys would drive something a little less close to the ground," I complained, "say a modest Rolls or a Daimler — something a lady with a sprained ankle could climb in and out of without so much loss of dignity."

They both smiled indulgently at my attempt to be witty, and Ali Reza said, "Not very grateful, your lady."

"She's hard to keep in line," Shaheen said, "but I like her that way." And with that we parted.

My chauffeur proved to be a more amusing companion than his somewhat heavy face and beetling black brows suggested. In fact, he talked all the way to Vallenjak in a wonderfully funny mixture of Farsi and English about his car, about his family, about his family's ridiculously extravagant villa in Niavarin. ("We have one point six bathrooms per person. This is five hundred percent the national average. I am economics at T.U. so I know these things. All gold-plated. You don't believe me but is true.") Soon he had me laughing helplessly, which was, no doubt, what he had intended, and I was in better shape to face my family when we arrived than I would have thought possible.

"Ali Reza, thank you," I said, when we pulled up at the door. "Please don't get out. I will make a better entrance on my own."

He frowned, then reached into the back of the car and produced a long umbrella. "Make a good walking stick," he said. "Take it. We have . . ." He paused, obviously in search of one last good story.

"I know," I said, "you have two thousand umbrellas, all gold-plated."

He looked surprised. "How do you guess so close?"

"I'm a witch," I said, and made my painful exit while he was still trying to figure that one out.

My reception was no better than might have been expected. My parents had heard about the rioting on the radio and naturally suspected the worst. I had ready a story of marginal involvement in the fringes of the disturbances and of a sensible but lengthy flight during which I had fallen into a *jube*, which accounted for my ankle and my bedraggled appearance. Whether any of this was believed is hard to say, but I stuck to it, and the need to minister to my physical plight soon gave at least my mother something else to think about. In a mercifully short time I found myself propped up in bed with an elastic bandage around my ankle and a bowl of chicken soup in my lap. As my father stood at the door to say good night, he echoed Shaheen in an even more pointed way: "Well, my little guerrilla," he said, "it will be good to know that you are out of action for a few days at least."

"That's fine with me too," I said. "Good night, Dad."

Chapter 25

The next three days were appalling. My father stayed home from work, explaining that his students would all be off marching in demonstrations and setting fire to things, and he didn't have the heart to sit at his desk while the oil company executives gathered round to complain about the perfidy of youth. My mother dug vigorously in the garden, but didn't seem to be getting any fun out of it. James moped and bewailed a "serious creative block" which prevented him from filling his time with his beloved paints and clay. Ali was off somewhere demonstrating with the religious contingent, who were now in full mourning for the martyrs of Tabriz.

For my part, I reclined tragically on the lavender couch with the telephone and the radio at my side. The radio gave me far more information than I wanted and the phone far less, though I must admit that Shaheen kept his word and called me at least twice a day. He seemed cheerful and full of energy, delighted, I thought, to be in the thick of the action and to have me out of the way.

Hundreds of thousands of people were marching and gathering in the streets of Tehran. The shah seemed at a loss, and his paralysis of will spread to the police who, like irritable dogs, snapped at the insurgent groups from time to time but seldom stayed to fight. Thus the revolutionaries were stung often enough to make them savage without being in the least intimidated. They roamed the city, overturning vehicles, breaking barricades, and burning banks. Some of this activity seemed pointless to me. "Why burn banks?" I asked. "It just makes a mess."

"To harry the establishment," Shaheen explained patiently.

I thought this over and decided to let it go. "Are you being shot at?" was my next and far more urgent question.

"Not much," Shaheen said. "Please don't worry. You can't make a pie without breaking any eggs."

"Omelet," I said automatically.

"What?"

"Omelet," I shrieked over the customary crackling and buzzing of the telephone line. "It's an omelet you can't make without breaking eggs. Shaheen, for heaven's sake what are we talking about? I'm worried out of my head about you. I can't move. Come and see me."

"I will, soon," he said. "Things are slowing down."

This was on the second day of my incarceration, and I could detect no signs of a slowdown in the murderous enthusiasm of either side.

By the third day, however, the crowds had shrunk, and from what little one could tell from the radio there seemed to be fewer incidents of incendiarism. It was April first. The weather was unbelievably beautiful, and I was hobbling around the garden when Shaheen called in the late afternoon.

He sounded tired and dispirited. "I'm afraid it's all going to fade out again," he said. "We'll have to retrench. Meanwhile I've just about had it. I'm exhausted."

"That's not surprising," I said. "Get some rest. I suspect you've made enough trouble for three or four men."

"Yes, well, it's depressing all the same," he said, "and I haven't been able to practice in days. That's something I wanted to talk to you about, Jill. I really can't handle the Beethoven now. I'll bring you the first horn part to study. You can do it beautifully."

"What are you talking about?" I cried. "That's absurd. Of course you can do it, and of course I can't. I couldn't possibly. I don't even want to."

He let me gabble on some more in this vein, and then he said, "April Fool, Jill!"

"Shaheen!" I said. "You are not even supposed to *know* about such things. You wretch! How could you?"

He was laughing now and sounded totally normal. "Got you," he said. "What a great success. Jill, tomorrow is the thirteenth of No Ruz, and I think almost everyone is going to lay down the torch and head for the country. This is the day when we are supposed to take our pots of *sabzi* and dump them in running water. Then everyone has a picnic, usually in the rain, but this year we seem to be in luck. Shall we try? We'll have to leave at around five a.m. to be ahead of the crowd. How's your ankle?"

"Great," I said. "Marvelous. That is, I can walk a few steps to some flowery bank with a lot of good strong support."

"That's all that will be required," he said. "See you at the crack of dawn then?"

"Absolutely. I'll pack a lunch — maybe a breakfast and a dinner too."

"Don't knock yourself out," he said. "We'll improvise. The main thing is to get together and get out."

With that sentiment I could not have agreed more.

Chapter 26

By six a.m. when we hit the road it was already clear that Tehran was in a state of evacuation. The normal morning flow of traffic had been reversed. Everyone except the very infirm and the very sensible was headed for the hills.

"Pity the poor mountains," I said to Shaheen as we waited for the light at the corner of Avenue Pahlavi, "having all this bad luck dumped on their innocent feet."

Shaheen smiled at me. "They can take it," he said. "Look at them."

The mountains, indeed, were as enormous and serene as ever, towering above the plane trees to our left. I felt as if I had been gone from their peaceful flanks for months rather than only a few days. The light changed, and Shaheen seized the gear stick. I shifted my grip from his hand to his knee. Ever since he had come in the door this morning, I had been unable to resist touching him — reassuring myself that he was here with me, real, alive, unchanged.

"The traffic will be horrendous later," he said, "but this picnic day will be good for people. When total revolution comes, there won't be much time for picnics."

"You're sure that it will come?" I asked, and he nodded vehemently.

"Now I am sure," he said. "Now that I've been out in the streets and felt the strength of the crowds. And you know, Jill, already some strange things are happening. We are less afraid of the army than we were. Yesterday a small group of soldiers refused to fire on the people. It was only one incident, but it was heartening. Khomeini tells us that we must offer ourselves as martyrs to the soldiers, and to call out to them as we fall that they are our brothers and that we have but one cause. He says, 'The blood of each martyr is a bell which will awaken a thousand of the living.'"

I stared at Shaheen and slowly withdrew my hand from his knee. I felt cold, as if I had touched him and found him already dead. And yet he had never seemed more alive. In the first rays of the morning sun his face was bright with the passion of conviction, and I thought that for all his western sophistication, the Iranian ideal of martyrdom had a powerful appeal even to him.

"Shaheen," I said, "you must fight for freedom and for social justice. The soldiers should be made to see that this is their battle too, because they are part of an oppressed people. But all this religious fervor makes my blood run cold."

"Oh it's not religious for me," he said. "You know that. But it's the same feeling. It must be. Only so are the great, unequal battles won."

"Yes," I said, "freedom fighters are always fanatics, and when they have won, they are still fanatics. This is what makes revolutions turn out so badly."

"You sound like your father," he said, and added quickly, "not that that is such a bad thing."

"Well, you can't expect the blood of martyrs to run in my

191

veins," I said, "but I want you to win, and I will do anything to help you. What can I do?"

"Nothing for the moment, love," he said, reaching out and recapturing my hand. "Just be my girl for a while, and I'll let you know if there's something more concrete."

"Maybe I could limp around handing out pamphlets," I suggested. "Who would suspect me?"

"Maybe you can," Shaheen said. "Meanwhile we are supposed to be carrying all the bad things from last year out of Tehran and dumping them in some babbling brook, so let's concentrate on that."

"Only good things happened to me last year," I said, "but I'll try to think of something."

We took the highway west out of Tehran and then turned into the foothills in the hope of finding some secluded and attractive valley that would call for a minimum of walking. This turned out to be not at all a simple matter, and I could see as we wound steadily upward that Shaheen was really very tired.

"You should have taken your holiday at home in bed," I said.

"Not without company," he said, his spirits briefly revived at the thought.

"Resting," I replied firmly.

"I shall sleep in your lap," he said, "if we ever find a place to put your lap."

Finally we settled for a place where a tiny stream came down from the hills and wound its way around the feet of three old walnut trees. Shaheen parked the car on the verge and helped me down the embankment, and we spread a blanket on a circle of grass that was hidden from the road by a thick tangle of wild rose bushes.

"Not that we won't be joined," Shaheen said gloomily.

"We would have to drive a hundred miles from the city today to find a place to ourselves this near the road."

"This is lovely," I said, "and it's small. Perhaps we'll be lucky. Anyway, have some fruit. You look as if you could use a second breakfast."

When we had eaten, I propped my back against a walnut tree, took off my shoes, and stretched my still wintry-looking legs in the sun. I was wearing a soft old denim skirt instead of jeans, in the hope of getting a little tan. It also made a better resting place for the head of my beloved, who promptly carried out his threat to fall asleep in my lap.

You might think this a dull way to spend a holiday. I did not find it so. I looked at the mountain peaks through the lacy branches of the trees and listened to the complicated language of the stream. A round brown bird like a quail, made bold by our silence, led her brood of six across the clearing and into the shelter of the rose. Soon I began to see the swift flicker of lizards among the rocks, and one came out and stretched itself in the sun almost at my feet.

Most of all, of course, I gazed down at Shaheen. He looked young and strangely innocent in spite of the thick black beard, and I thought of the revolution and of Khomeini's thirst for martyrs. "They can't have him," I said to myself. "It's not right. No cause is worth this sacrifice." But I knew that I was probably wrong and that anyway, it didn't matter what I thought. Young men had died for centuries, and I supposed the lucky ones were the ones who died for something for which they cared with this consuming passion. So many gave their lives for no reason at all.

I had plenty of time to think as well of topics which were more personal and less grim. In this I was stimulated but not helped by Shaheen who, from time to time, smiled happily in his sleep and burrowed deeper into my lap. When would we sleep together? Where? What would it be like? This was no longer a debate, if it ever seriously had been. Now every nerve in my body cried out for it to come. Shaheen stirred again, this time more vigorously and, turning on his side, slid one hand up under my skirt to a cozy resting place on my upper thigh. This felt extremely good and took my mind off a growing problem I was having with the circulation in my lower legs. It also made me quiver from head to foot like an aspen leaf.

The sun rose higher and began to burn my shins. Then came the sound of a car stopping on the edge of the road, followed by voices and laughter. I gave Shaheen a shake. "Time to get up," I said. "We're about to have company, and besides, I think I am paralyzed from the waist down."

He sat up groggily and glared at a large Iranian family that was struggling down the embankment with huge hampers and shopping bags full of food. They came to rest on the opposite side of the stream and began to spread out a formidable feast. Melons and bottles of Coke went into the water to cool. These were followed by a large pot of *sabzi*, the hundreds of green shoots shining in the sun as they broke apart and swirled away in the current.

"We should have brought ours," Shaheen said. "I suppose my mother pitched it in the *jube*."

"That's what we did with ours," I said, "but I hated to see it go."

"Well, it would be scandalous to keep it," he said. "Ali would have done it for you, if you hadn't. Why don't those people move upstream a little? My countrymen are too gregarious."

"Be grateful that we had the morning to ourselves," I said. "Anyway, if they are from Tehran, they probably feel that an ocean of space separates our two picnics. The children are

194

darling, but can't the little girl take off her chador even out here?"

"She could if she wanted to. If it were hotter, she would probably go swimming in it." Shaheen stood up, yawning and stretching, and ambled down to the stream to retrieve our wine. He stood on the bank for a moment and greeted the family across the water while I waved to the children from where I sat.

"Will they mind if we drink wine?" I asked when Shaheen had returned to our blanket.

He grinned cynically. "We'd just better drink it fast," he said, "before the men come over for a little hospitality."

No one, however, attempted to join us, and we had our lunch in some privacy, the others being absorbed in a spread that was surely fit for a Qajar prince and his court.

"Time for another nap," Shaheen said cheerfully when we had packed up the remains, but I shook my head.

"I really don't think so," I said. "While you slumber blissfully with your arms around my legs, I may have trouble sitting here looking like your albino sister. Let's limp up the stream a bit and then go home. Maybe we'll be ahead of the worst of the traffic."

And so we walked a little, using my evident lameness as an excuse for arms tightly wrapped around each other. Then we joined the stream of picnickers on the road back to Tehran. Thus ended the thirteenth and last day of No Ruz, a day of peace that we would look back upon with longing during the stormy weeks that lay ahead.

Chapter 27

The holidays were now officially over.
Most people went back to work, and we went back to school.
But the spirit of protest in Tehran did not die out as it had
after the riots in Qom and Tabriz. Rather it sank to an uneasy
simmer, punctuated almost every day by an explosion of
some kind, usually a literal explosion as the dissidents took
out another bank or lobbed a hand grenade at a passing police car. Still, Tehran was a vast city; and the middle-class
foreigners in their peaceful hillside villas did not appear to
feel nervous about going downtown to work or sending their
children off in buses to remote schools. The shah had ruled
so long that hardly anyone could really comprehend the
shakiness of his regime.

My sprained ankle had served me well in one respect. For
want of anything better to do, I had been practicing like a
fiend. Not so Shaheen, nor, it would seem, many of the other players. Helmut was absent and I looked accusingly at
Shaheen. "What did you do to Helmut?" I asked.

"Nothing yet," he said, laughing. "It's just a happy coincidence. Move up and take advantage of it."

Mr. Perenyi warmed us up with a Sousa march, then,

sweeping us all with a look of passionate hopefulness, called for the "Egmont" Overture. It was a catastrophe. What did he expect after a two-week vacation? The only pleasant surprise was Jill Alexander substituting on second horn, and this was hardly enough to gladden a conductor's heart. The woodwinds, with their thankless task of trying to sound like forty or fifty symphonic string players, were more than usually out of tune. The trumpets and trombones overblew as if they were coming down the football field at the half with a bunch of lusty cheerleaders to spur them on.

Since some of our entrances were in unison, I partly covered the other horns. There remained, however, plenty of places for the first to mess it up alone, and none of these opportunities was missed.

Finally Mr. Perenyi could bear no more. He stopped us with a gesture of tragic finality and snapped his baton in two. Probably no one in the Tehran Community School band had ever seen a conductor do this before, but no one laughed. "May God, in his infinite mercy, deliver me from these imbecilic *children*," our beloved leader cried, as we sat cowering with our instruments in our laps. He gazed at us somberly for a while longer, his fingers gradually loosening their grip on the broken ends of his baton. Then he gave the faintest of smiles. "Well?" he said. "Are you sorry? Will you go home and practice?" We nodded dumbly. "Or do I have to resign and leave this lovely city under a cloud?" We shook our heads.

Now Mr. Perenyi focused on Shaheen, his pride and joy. "I wonder," he said, "if you know the story of this beautiful music — the story of Egmont — do you?"

Shaheen stared at him, fascinated. "Not really," he mumbled.

"It is the story of a great revolutionary," the conductor said

197

softly, "of the Count of Egmont who gave his life to free the oppressed people of Flanders in the sixteenth century. He died, but, as you can hear in the triumphant closing passages of the overture, his cause prevailed, and the Flemish people won their liberty."

Shaheen had gone quite pale. "I see," he said in a barely audible voice. "I'm glad you told me that."

"So!" shouted Mr. Perenyi, with a return to his usual ebullient spirits. "You will all go home and practice, and I will go out and buy a new baton, and tomorrow it will be a different story. Eh?"

We scrambled to our feet with relief, although the hour was only about half over, and went out into the spring sunshine.

"It occurs to me for the first time," I said to Shaheen, "that Mr. Perenyi was probably a Hungarian freedom fighter."

Shaheen looked even more stricken than before. "And here he is, an exile, his country in chains, his only reward a bunch of lazy and incompetent high school band players."

"Oh, come," I said. "Let's not go overboard. He strikes me as a very cheerful and energetic man who enjoys his work. A little temperament is becoming to a Middle European musician. He probably knew we would sound terrible today. The touch of drama was just to make sure that tomorrow would be a whole lot better. He certainly knew how to get at you, though. I have to hand it to him."

"You'll regret those words while you ride the bus," Shaheen said. "I'm going home to practice."

Chapter 28

That April, which began so peacefully be-
side a mountain stream, developed into one of the two most
traumatic months in my entire life. The other one was May.
Everything happened pretty much all at the same time, and
almost none of it was good.

My mother and I were the first members of the family to
learn that my father had lost his job at the oil company. That
is, we learned of it before my father did and in a manner
which was typical of the convoluted and conspiratorial nature
of Tehran society.

We were in the garden one beautiful, bright afternoon
when Mr. Fahouri slid around the corner of the house. After
greeting my mother with the usual courtesies, he began to
explain something in Farsi.

"Jill, help, I need a translator," she called, so I joined
them at the edge of the flower bed.

"Since Agha Iskander is not at home," Mr. Fahouri said,
with an overtone of wonder that this should be the case on
a Monday afternoon, "I have asked the *khanoum* to tell him
that I would like the rent for May."

"Please tell me, Agha," I said, as politely as I could manage, "why you would like the rent for May when it is not yet the middle of April."

He had the grace to look uncomfortable. "I am a business man," he said, "and a poor man besides. I have many debts. I must protect myself."

"Protect yourself against what?" I asked more sharply.

"Since your father is no longer in the employ of Naft Melli, I must ask myself if the money will be available. If not, with great regret, I must make other plans," he said.

For a moment the sun seemed to go dark, and my head swam. As if at a great distance I could hear my mother imploring me to explain. I turned to her. "He has some cock and bull story about Dad not being at the oil company any more," I said.

My mother was evidently not swept with the foreboding which possessed me. She knew Iran less well than I. "That's ridiculous," she said, and then, summoning her limited Farsi, "My husband is at Naft Melli now. This minute."

Mr. Fahouri shook his head. "Often, I fear, the employee is the last to know."

"Agha Fahouri," I said, "I am unable to understand what this shameful gossip has to do with the payment of your rent. It will, of course, be paid in full and at the proper time, which is the beginning of May."

"I must have assurances. I will speak to your father tonight," he said, beginning a crablike exit from the garden.

"Please do," I said coldly, and turned my back on his departure.

When he had gone, I made a dive for the house and the telephone, knowing that my mother would only stand there and argue that such a thing was impossible in a civilized country. What made her think she was in a civilized country? After trying all eight numbers for the oil company, I finally got through on the eighth. No, my father had not heard that he was fired, but he didn't sound so surprised as I had hoped. "Things are a little uneasy here," he said. "Rumors are flying, but that's nothing new. I'll check into it. Don't worry, Jill."

"Who, me worry?" I said with a ghastly laugh and, hanging up the phone, collapsed into the lavender chair. I stared at the cool, tranquil spaces of our living room, at the Rohanis' beautiful rug, at the great shoulders of the mountains rising behind the houses across the street; and I knew that it was true, that the curtain was slowly coming down on my life in Iran.

My father came home early. I went out to meet him and could see from his face as he climbed out of the car that my worst fears were confirmed. He put his arm around me, and we walked into the house.

"Don't look like that," he said. "It may not be so bad." He threw his briefcase and jacket on the couch where my mother was sitting, twisting her hands in her lap and looking up at him with an imploring face. "Now look," he said, "all that has really happened so far is that my classes have been suspended because there has been a so-called change of policy. Funds have been reallocated to areas which it is felt will be more beneficial to Iranian oil production, etcetera, etcetera. Certainly some other use will be found for my invaluable services. Meanwhile, why don't I take a nice vacation — see something of the country. When I come back, they will have thought of something for me to do. Unofficially, of course, the story is quite different. My classes are thought to be hotbeds of radical plotting which I have actively encouraged. There are dark hints of Communist connections in my past. Certainly the students like me far too well. Miss Hikmet has reported that some of them even call me by my first name. In short, I am an undesirable person, but this doesn't mean that they won't find something else for me to do — something harmless to occupy me until the expiration of my contract."

"Something which you wouldn't even consider doing," I said bitterly, "no matter how much we might want to stay in Iran, no matter how well you were being paid."

"I will certainly consult with the rest of you if an offer is made," he said. "Don't I always?"

"Oh, you always consult with us," I replied, "but as for doing some kind of work you don't believe in just to make us happy, that's another story."

My mother spoke for the first time. She was not, perhaps, the most practical member of the family, but she was the one who had to buy the groceries. "Speaking of money," she said. "With what are we supposed to take this interesting vacation?"

"I was told that in a few days I would receive a check for the first half of April," my father said.

I jumped to my feet. "So that's it," I cried. "They really are through with you, or you would be paid at the end of the month just like every other time. I knew it. All the rest is just talk, talk, talk."

"And what are we supposed to do with twenty-five hundred dollars?" my mother asked. "Mr. Fahouri wants the rent for May, and that's more than half of it right there."

"Well, he's not going to get it," my father said angrily. "And be calm, both of you. You know perfectly well that if this job really is terminated, I get two months' severance pay and moving expenses and airline tickets and I don't know what else."

The mention of airline tickets was the final blow for me.

"I won't go!" I shouted. "You can go. I'm staying right here."

"Jill, you can't," my mother cried. "Where would you live?"

"She knows perfectly well she can't," he said in a reasonable voice which only enraged me further. "It's just a reaction, and an understandable one at that. Now please, both of you, don't start packing or saying any tragic farewells. It can probably all be worked out with the oil company so that I do some less sensitive but entirely satisfactory work, or I may even find a private client. Lots of people have been interested in my services during the past year."

"Well, they won't be now," I said, "and don't try to encourage me or insult my intelligence. I'm going out."

I plunged out of the house and up the road, walking blindly, seeing nothing but the desolation in my mind. Asef with its white houses and blossoming trees, the heartbreaking beauty of the mountains, the people I passed, all might have been a thousand miles away. Only one scene rose before my eyes — the grim departure lounge of Mehrabad Airport where Shaheen and I would embrace for the last time. It was too much. I walked faster and faster until suddenly I realized that I was above Vallenjak, by the little bridge over the mountain stream. And there at last I sat down and wept. It was growing dark when I finally stumbled to my feet. Normally I would have been a bit scared of walking down through the village in the dusk. Now, however, my only thought was to get home and call Shaheen.

But the living room seemed to be full of people all talking and gesticulating at once. In fact, there were only five — my parents and Mr. Fahouri, who were screaming at each other in Farsi, and James and Ali, who were listening. James looked pale, but Ali had the avid expression of one who thrives on bad news for its dramatic value in an otherwise tedious life. I stood and listened just inside the door since the last thing I wanted was to be called in as an interpreter.

Our landlord was explaining how poor he was. He had apparently lost a packet gambling and had bought one too many BMWs for his womenfolk. These indiscretions brought no tears to the eyes of my parents who were, through no fault of their own, nearly penniless in a foreign land. The conversation went round and round, from Mr. Fahouri's demands to my mother's exclamations of outrage, to my father's adamant refusals. Mr. Fahouri said he would call the police. My father said he should do just that. Ali looked petrified.

Linguistically, of course, my parents were at a serious disadvantage. My mother's Farsi improved in moments of stress, but my father's deteriorated badly, which brought them about even. The Farsi word for "go" is *boro;* the word for "come" is *bia.* For some reason Dad sometimes confused the two in moments of high emotion. Now he gathered himself to his formidable height and delivered his peroration. "This is still my house, Agha Fahouri," he announced. "It is not your house. "So, *BIA!*"

To do him credit, Mr. Fahouri was not confused. He left, grumbling and threatening, but still going, not coming. Ali ducked into the kitchen in a paroxysm of mirth.

"Oh my God, I've done it again," my father shouted in English, and we all laughed, our pent-up emotions breaking into hilarity. "Jill," Dad said, seeing me for the first time, "how long have you been here? Why didn't you come to my rescue?"

"You seemed to be handling it so well," I said, and started laughing again.

After James and Mum had gone off to the bedroom wing,

I went and perched on the arm of my father's chair. "Are you really thinking of going home right away?" I asked.

He put his free arm around my waist and stared somberly out across the living room. "Not immediately, Jill," he said, "maybe not for a long time, but I can't make any promises. You know that. We have to take each day as it comes and hope for the best. I do feel, as you obviously do not, that Iran is becoming a rather undesirable place to be; but I would like to help these kids, and I would like to see what they do. Also, I am not really anxious to break the heart of my only daughter, you know."

I bent and leaned my cheek against his. "Yes," I said, "I do know. I'm sorry about what I said before."

"No, you had a right, and there's some truth in what you said. My work is enormously important to me, and I expect my family to adjust to whatever demands I may make upon it. That's not fair, but you are all so wonderfully elastic."

"I think this time I have been stretched just a wee bit too far," I said as lightly as I could, and giving his arm a gentle squeeze, I went off to my room before another surge of emotion could overtake me. It seemed hopeless now to call Shaheen — too difficult with my father sitting right by the phone, too difficult altogether. I wanted more than anything to see him, but that would have to wait until tomorrow.

Chapter 29

The school day seemed interminable, and even though I saw Shaheen in band, I wanted to wait until we were in the car to give him the bad news. There wasn't, after all, very much to say, but I hadn't been sure what effect the saying of it would have on me. A flood of tears in the band room I felt would be less than helpful to both of us. "My father's lost his job," I said, as soon as the car doors were closed.

Shaheen stopped with his hand on the ignition. "It had to happen," he said. "I should have known when I saw your face."

For a long moment we just sat there staring straight ahead. Then he turned and reached for my hands. As I felt his fingers wind around mine, I closed my eyes trying to keep back the tears. "I'm not going to cry," I said almost angrily. "We may not even have to go. Everything is horribly confused and up in the air." I groped for a tissue to stem the flow.

"Tell me about it," Shaheen said. So we sat in the car in the narrow street, holding hands, oblivious of the stream of students and Tehrani flowing by, and I told him everything that had happened the day before.

"Typical," Shaheen said when I had finished.

"What do you mean, typical?" I asked. It was somehow not the reaction I had expected.

He spread his hands and brought them down hard on the steering wheel. "The whole damn scene is so familiar — so inevitable," he said. "That fat Fahouri should have heard it on the grapevine, that there are at least two versions and probably a dozen sub-versions of what is going on at the oil company, all the waffling and vague promises which will come to nothing. It's typical and it's disgusting."

"At the moment," I said sharply, "I am not interested in this as an Iranian phenomenon. What I care about is what it means to you and me."

He turned an anguished face to me and took my hand again. "Oh Jill, I know," he said. "What are we going to do?"

It was my turn to be controlled. "Live from day to day, as my father says."

"Have you got enough money?" he asked, surprising me again.

"Oh what does it matter?" I cried. "Yes, I suppose so. At least until the end of the month, and if we really are finished here, Naft Melli will have to give us a pile of compensation. This is really the least of my worries."

"I hope it will stay that way," Shaheen said gloomily.

"I don't care if we starve," I said passionately, "and old Fahouri can send the national guard for his rent for all I care. I just don't want to go home."

"I'll speak to my father," he said. "Maybe he'll have a bright idea. He knows vast numbers of people, though more in the bazaar than in government or industry. I can't think what anyone in the bazaar would want with an oil engineer, but you never can tell." He started the car and nosed out into the traffic.

The thought of Agha Rohani — handsome, urbane, exuding silent power — made me smile for the first time. I, too, doubted if there was much he could do for an American employee of the National Oil Company, but the thought of having him on our side was comforting.

We drove for a long time without speaking. The radio, as if conspiring to break my heart, was tuned to an Iranian station, and I listened to the voice of the *tar* spin out what was surely some tale of separation and terrible grief. I stared at the ugly, crowded streets of Tehran and at last I said, "It beats me how anyone can mourn for such a ghastly place."

Shaheen smiled faintly. "Tehran has its hidden charms, as you well know, and besides, it's more what happens to a person in a place that counts, isn't it?"

"How love transforms the universe," I said sardonically. "But, you know, it had begun to grow on me even before I met you. God knows why."

"Many people love Tehran," he answered. "As you say, God knows why."

When we reached the expressway and the mountains rose before us in all their glory, I could feel my control slipping again. "Of course, I knew I would have to go in the fall," I said, "but I wanted to have the summer here, and I was hoping you would be coming too — at least to the same continent."

"But Jill, I will come," he said. "Maybe even this fall. It depends how fast things move." He gave me one of his best smiles, which made me feel distinctly worse, and I shook my head stubbornly.

"I think it will go on and on," I said, "and there I'll be never knowing if you are safe or what is happening or anything." Several large tears rolled down my face, and I let them roll.

"You mustn't cry all the time," Shaheen said. "I really can't stand it."

"What do you mean?" I said indignantly. "I haven't been crying all the time. You haven't seen anything yet. You're just going to have to get used to it. I'm a crier."

"No, you are not," Shaheen said firmly.

"Yes, I am too," I said, and started laughing through my tears.

When we arrived at the house, Shaheen got his horn out of the back of the car. "I'll just have a look at that Haydn concerto, if you don't mind," he mumbled. "Maybe I want to borrow it."

I nodded numbly, and we trudged through the living room with a nod to my mother, who looked up at us from her book with tragic eyes as if we were Romeo and Juliet marching to our well-known doom. We went into my room and closed the door. Our horns went onto the floor and we into each other's arms. The tears were pouring down my cheeks again, but I closed my eyes tightly against them as I kissed Shaheen, and he stroked my hair and didn't tell me not to cry. We played no duets, and Shaheen forgot to look at the Haydn, if he had ever meant to do so. When he went home, I felt better, though my face was a wreck and caused more anguished glances from my softhearted mother.

"It's all *right*," I said. "We'll probably survive. Just please, don't look that way."

She nodded, her face still full of misery, and I left her there, thinking, Life is bad enough, isn't it, without having to comfort your parents too?

Chapter 30

A few nights later the Enrights came over to commiserate and complain. Tedious though they were, it was comforting to talk things over with other Americans. They assumed that we would be leaving as soon as we could get ourselves together and found my father's search for other work in Iran nearly incomprehensible.

Bob Enright settled into a corner of the couch with a glass of our hoarded Scotch in his hand and prepared to expound. "My God, George," he said. "Count yourself lucky. The company will have to pay you double for giving you the boot, and you'll be out of this hole. It was bad enough before the kids started blowing things up. Now when you want to cash a check, you never know whether your branch will be a pile of rubble or not."

"And it's not as if any other branch would do it for you," my father said seriously.

"That's right," Marjorie said, "I nearly flipped when I found that out."

"It's not so safe for the girls any more either," Bob went

on, and I wondered if this had just occurred to him and if James, thanks to his membership in the male fraternity, was mysteriously immune to bombs and grenades.

"I worry night and day," Marjorie contributed.

My father said that Tehran had come to have a certain gruesome fascination for us, and I looked up to find Barbara's eyes boring into my face. Of course, everybody knew why I didn't want to leave Iran. It was the motivation of the rest of the family that was puzzling. I felt grateful to Barbara for not saying something of the sort and suddenly thought that it would be nice to talk to her alone in my room as we used to do.

"Come on, Barb," I said. "Let's leave these people to the post mortem and play some music."

She jumped up happily. Once in my room, however, I felt at a loss for words and bumbled around silently looking for a tape to play. Barbara curled up on the bed and watched me with unnerving intensity until I finally settled on Janis Ian and the tape began to play on my creaky old cassette machine. Then she made the obvious remark. "It must be hell for you," she said.

"You could say that these are not the brightest days of my life," I answered. Now that we were together I felt a perverse desire to be cool and uncommunicative.

"But Shaheen will be coming over to school in the fall, won't he?" she went on. "I mean, I'm sure you hate to miss the summer together, but it's not that long, and Boston's not that far from Providence."

I shook my head. "I doubt very much that he'll be coming in the fall. The revolution is getting hotter every day. He would never leave while so much was going on."

"Revolution, bullshit," Barbara said. "There isn't any rev-

211

olution except in your heads — just a bunch of kids who think they're tough playing with bombs. When the shah gets really tired of it, he'll squash it like a gnat. I can't imagine why he hasn't already."

"Exactly," I said. "Nobody can imagine why he hasn't done it, and every day he fails to move, the opposition gets stronger and his people get weaker. You think you know a lot, but really all you know is what you hear other Americans say, and all they know is what they hear each other say. But I've been out in the streets with Shaheen when it was all happening, and I've met some of his friends. They're not playing cops and robbers, I promise you."

"You've actually been in the street riots?" Barbara asked, impressed in spite of herself.

"Only one," I admitted, "but it was quite an experience. That's how I sprained my ankle — not running away as the story goes, but doing something else, I don't remember what — something to do with pushing over a truckful of riot police I think it was. Unfortunately," I went on, "Shaheen leaves me out of as much of the excitement as he can. Going to a riot is just not his idea of a date. He's old-fashioned that way."

"You really are crazy," Barbara said. "Crazy period and crazy about that guy. I almost envy you."

"Don't," I said briefly.

Barbara looked wistful. "I think it would be fabulous to love someone that much."

"Fabulous," I said, "fabled as in song and story. Only the songs and stories always seem to have such sad endings. That's the other side of the coin."

"Still," she said, "it will be something to remember."

"You could say that."

"Are you sleeping together?" Barbara asked suddenly, as if it was the most natural question in the world. Maybe to her it was.

I gave her a fishy look. "I think I'll pass on that one," I said.

"That means you are," she said, then gave me a doubtful glance. "Or else it means you're not . . ."

"Take your pick," I said.

"I used to think I could read your mind," she complained, "but not any more."

"Much better that way," I said, "and anyway, I can't help it. I often want to let down my hair, but when the chance comes, I find I really don't want to after all. I'm sorry. That's just the way it is."

"It's not good to keep things all bottled up."

"Privacy," I said. "In Tehran I have discovered what a wonderful thing it is, maybe because it's so rare."

"Well I give up," Barbara said, "and shut off that dreary music. It's making me want to cry, and I don't have anything to cry about except roasting through another Tehran summer without a swimming pool."

I switched off the tape. "So find something cheerful. It's not all that easy."

Barbara started looking through my cassettes while I got up and prowled around the room. I picked up my horn and twiddled the valves, thinking that if she would go, I could practice. It seemed to do me more good than anything lately, certainly more than this stupid conversation.

Barbara held up a Mozart symphony. "Aside from classical I can't seem to find anything that doesn't involve a lot of grief in one way or another," she said. "Is this okay?"

"Terrific," I said, "and cheerful besides, but not on my

machine. Let's go get something to drink and enjoy it in golden silence."

Barbara jumped at this chance to get out of my room, and I'm afraid we were both delighted to find our parents on their feet and drifting toward the door.

"There you are, Barbie," her mother called out. "I was just about to look for you. Have a nice chat?"

"Super," Barbara said, and I winced thinking, well, there goes my best friend. A lot of good we are to each other now. A lot of good I am to anyone for that matter, except Shaheen. Except Shaheen. I waved to the departing guests and scrambled back to my room to practice.

Chapter 31

Following the depressing evening with the Enrights, there was a sort of lull in our affairs, but it was a lull so charged with uncertainty that it could hardly be described as peaceful.

Among other things, we were running out of money. The oil company had paid the promised sum for the first two weeks of April, and my parents had, with more virtue than wisdom, paid some bills with most of it. The voracious jaws of Iran Super soon closed over the remainder. Now we began to haunt the bazaar in search of bargains and ran up a bill with the friendly Turkomans who kept the small grocery store on Asef. Dad turned in the car, which meant that everyone became a belated virtuoso in the art of orange-cabbing.

One obvious budgetary cut was to rid ourselves of Ali. While we were gathering our strength for the inevitable scene, however, Ali received the news that he had been drafted. I found him in the living room one day in his characteristic posture of despair, shoulders hunched, face buried in his hands. When he looked up at me, I was horrified to see that his cheeks were wet with tears. "Oh Missus Jill," he sobbed, "I am soldier no!" and held out an official looking document. It would have taken me a month to read the thing, but it wasn't hard to put two and two together and come up with the fate of poor Ali. For the first time in all the months that he had lived in our house I felt truly sorry for him. "That's terrible, Ali," I said in Farsi. "The Iranian army must be really unpleasant, especially now with all the troubles."

"I will not shoot my brothers!" he said suddenly, vehemently. "If the Shah-an-Shah asks me to shoot my brothers, I will put a rose in my rifle barrel so everyone can see what I think, and I will go to prison."

My sympathy flickered briefly into actual liking, although it seemed to me that his personality was not improved by heroics. Chiefly I thought, what an awful thing to happen to anyone — to have to be a soldier in Iran at any time. "Maybe the revolutionaries will win before you have to go," I said. "I hope they will."

It was clear in any event that going servantless was not going to be one of our economies. Financial relief was supposedly just around the corner — there for the asking in the coffers of Naft Melli. For a time my father's natural optimism and faith in his fellow man prevented him from cutting the last tenuous tie with the oil company and asking for his severance pay. When he finally brought himself to do it, he was promised a princely check amid protestations of sorrow that everything had not worked out better. We were relieved if saddened by the finality of this parting and settled in to wait while Dad continued to pursue the elusive hope of other Iranian employment. Neither the check nor the airline tickets appeared, however, and our meals became daily more imaginative and bizarre as we scrounged in the depths of the freezer for improbable but nourishing combinations.

216

Shaheen and I spent more time together than ever, in spite of the resurgence of unrest in the city as the simmering weeks of April moved toward the rolling boil of May. He seemed to care less for demonstrating than he had. "The revolution is not going to go away," he said tersely, leaving unspoken the thought that I almost certainly was. It was becoming clear that the only remaining questions were when and how we were going.

All of this probably sounds more dreadful than it really was. For one thing, the shocks, hopes, and disappointments were spread out and interspersed with the normal joys of living. And the joys of living were heightened by the seeming imminence of the end. Everything took on a special brilliance. The rosy flanks of the Alborz shimmered in the soft, clear air. The flowers, which my mother tended more ferociously than ever, seemed to spring overnight from the dark soil to spill a profusion of color against the gray garden wall. I touched and marveled at the mysterious diversity of unfurling shapes as the old fig tree came into full leaf. Shaheen and I did everything, not as if for the last time, but more in a spirit of celebration that yet one more day glimmered ahead.

The rapid approach of the spring band concert raised the emotional temperature a few more degrees. I told my parents firmly that no matter what happened I was not going to leave until I had played the "Egmont" Overture, and they, having no more idea than I about what would happen when, agreed. Shaheen insisted that I practice both second and third horn parts, and one day about two weeks before the concert, I came into the rehearsal room to find Helmut sitting in my accustomed place. I stood between the two stands wondering what to do. Finally I said, "Helmut, which one of us is confused?"

He gazed up at me blandly through his thick glasses. "I hope you do not object?" he said. "It is too long since I have high horn played."

"But, but . . ." I said. "It's really a much smaller part and . . ."

Helmut shrugged amiably. "I have tried to take first horn," he explained, "but Shaheen is not — how do you say? — agreeable?"

I nodded, laughing. "I'm sure he's not," I said, "and I also suspect some sort of plot, but whatever the reason, I am very grateful, Helmut. As you probably know," I added, sitting down at the second stand, "I am likely to be leaving soon, so this is a nice going-away present."

For some reason these remarks caused Helmut to blush furiously. "I do not understand this word 'plot,'" he muttered.

"You understand it as well as I do, but thanks anyway," I said and turned smiling to Shaheen who was watching the exchange with a sardonic glint in his eye.

Mr. Perenyi rapped sharply with his baton. "If the young aristocrats of the horn section have decided where they are going to sit," he said mildly, "perhaps we could begin?" And we flung ourselves into another frenzied battle with Beethoven.

Chapter 32

As the days went by, it began to seem that I need not have worried about being on hand for the concert. Nothing was moving on the money front at all. The Alexander family grew hungrier and uncharacteristically tense. It was hard to know what to do.

Meanwhile the violence in the city increased from day to day. It began to seem that not even the most religious of the insurgents were going to wait another forty days to make their feelings known, and indeed, after the beginning of May there was no more peace in Iran. Reports of rioting in other cities arrived daily. Tehran itself seethed with fury as thousands of students and Moslem fanatics marched, demonstrated, and blew things up. Still the shah's government and its American advisers refused to admit that there was anything seriously wrong. As the situation worsened both at home and in the streets, I was torn between my longing to stay with Shaheen and an intense desire to see the last of Tehran.

It was in this highly charged atmosphere and only forty-eight hours before the concert that Shaheen was arrested. James had already left to catch the bus, and I was just walking out the door when the phone rang. I answered and heard his voice sounding both very young and also abnormally collected.

"Jill, thank God you're still there," he said. "Now listen. Don't panic but listen. I am being held by the Tajrish police for writing slogans on the wall of the bazaar. You know the sort of thing we do sometimes. Are you still there?"

"I'm here, Shaheen," I said faintly. I had, in fact, folded up at the knees and was kneeling by the telephone, shaking from head to foot. "Go on," I added in as firm a voice as I could manage.

"All right then. Good," he said, as if the fact that I was still on the telephone was a real advantage. "Now look," he went on, "they only let me make one call, so I chose you because I knew you wouldn't have hysterics. So far I have been treated fairly decently, but I will probably be moved to some more unpleasant place tonight. God knows where. So if anything is to be done, it has to be soon. It's probably hopeless, but see if you can reach my father in the bazaar. Maybe he can pull a few strings while I'm still where I can be found."

"Shaheen, wait a minute!" I cried, terrified that he might hang up, leaving me almost as much in the dark as I had been when he called. "Tell me what happened! I have to know. What were you doing? Who else was there? What are you charged with?"

"I'm not charged with anything so far," he said, "but I suppose it will be subversive activities or something of the sort — not a very good thing these days. And we were writing on the walls, or had just finished. Hossein, Ali Reza, Leila, Fatima, to answer your second question."

"And they all got away?" I asked incredulously. "Only you got caught?"

"I'm afraid they scattered and I didn't," he admitted.

"So they don't know who really did it?" I asked. I was catching at straws, trying to keep him on the line, wondering what his captors must think of his prolonged conversation in English.

"It had to be us, but it didn't have to be me," he said.

"What did you write?"

"Just 'Down with the shah,'" Shaheen said in a low voice, and then went on with more spirit, "If I had known it was to be my last slogan, I would have thought of something more original."

"Stop it," I said. "Don't talk that way. I'm trying to think."

Now, however, I could hear voices in the background, and Shaheen said something angrily in Farsi, then, "I can't say any more, Jill. Call my father. Don't worry," and the line went dead.

Don't worry. Don't panic. Of course not. I put down the phone and started to walk the floor, thankful that my parents were still back in the bedroom wing, oblivious to the crisis and thus unable to offer any advice until I got my feelings sorted out.

It would be at least two hours before I could call Agha Rohani at his shop in the bazaar, and obviously Shaheen had not wanted me to call him at home. Really, I thought, this was hardly the time to worry about alarming the womenfolk, but perhaps he had a better reason. Maybe his mother would do something that could cause more harm than good. How could I know?

Suddenly it occurred to me that I did not know how to call Agha Rohani. The vast city of Tehran has no telephone book for the excellent reason that people sell their telephone lines to each other every time they move, and the resulting confusion means that about half of the phone book would be out of date as soon as it was printed. There was an information service of sorts, if I could summon the psychic strength to try to use it. I gritted my teeth and dialed the code. After about thirty rings, a hostile voice asked how it could serve me. My request was simple, my Farsi clear. The operator, however, on hearing a foreign accent, immediately decided that communication was impossible and hung up. I hadn't expected anything different, but the frustration was almost too much. I flung myself down on the rug, then had an inspiration and started crawling around the edge of it looking to see if there might be a tag of some sort with the carpet shop's telephone number. This was what I was doing when my father came into the living room.

"What ho," he said, "counting the knots again?"

I sat back on my heels and looked at him with a face that must have warned him against any further jollity.

"Dad," I said. "Shaheen's been taken by the police."

His face went suddenly old and gray. "Where is he? What did he do?" he asked.

I crouched in the middle of the rug and told him what I knew. The morning sun had begun to slant in the east window, picking out the field of blue and purple flowers on which I sat. I was beginning to shake again and couldn't seem to do anything about it.

Dad stood and stared down at me. "The civil police," he muttered. "That's better than it might be, but as you say, it probably won't last. What the hell can we do? If only he were an American, and even then, he'd be in bad, bad trouble. I'm not trying to frighten you, Jill, but —"

"If I were any more frightened, I'd be dead," I said. "Don't worry about my state of mind."

"What a stupid, goddamn thing to do!" Dad shouted.

"What was the point? Why didn't he save his strength to use where it would count?"

I didn't answer this tirade, understanding it for what it was, an expression of impotent rage. "You don't know anyone," I asked timidly, "anyone at all? You know so many people."

"I know all the wrong people," he said. "I know people on the one side who would think shooting was too good for him, and I know people who, but for the grace of God, would be right there in the clink with him. But let me think. We need both power and secret sympathy. I probably know several such men, but how to identify them, reach them, and then maneuver them into doing something all in a few hours. That's the problem."

I felt a tiny spark of hope, which shows just how hard up I was. "Maybe if you went to Naft Melli, something would dawn on you," I said. "Maybe you would see someone who would remind you of someone else. It's the only thing I can think of. Oh, and while you're there, get some nice Iranian to call information and get the number of the Rohani carpet place and call me back. I thought maybe it would be on the underside of this thing, but no such luck."

"That at least I can do," he said and went back to the bedroom for his jacket.

He gave me a brief squeeze as he went out the door. "I haven't told your mother," he said. "Maybe you should."

"Later," I said briefly and watched him striding up toward Asef in search of an orange cab.

After he had gone, I stood by the front window staring out at the familiar scene but not seeing it — seeing instead a parade of horrific, half-formed images drawn, I suppose, from films and books, for my American life had not prepared me for the abyss that yawned in my imagination. I saw Shaheen, slender, defiant, but surely very much afraid, locked in a cell, handcuffed? beaten? My mind refused to follow this track any further, although I had heard enough tales of SA-VAK's prisons. "Well, he isn't there yet," I muttered angrily and began to pace the floor again. Then I thought, if my mother comes in, I simply won't be able to deal with it. I decided to spend the time before I could reasonably expect news from my father out of doors instead of fretting in the house.

When I reached Asef, I turned downhill. This was so contrary to my usual practice that I think my feet must already have known the crazy thing I was going to do. Certainly my head didn't have a clue. I passed the barbari bread oven, the dry cleaner, the little grocery of the friendly Turkomans. I stopped where the thick plane trees shaded the fruit and vegetable store to scratch the budding horns of the half-grown goat that was gorging itself on cast-off lettuce leaves. "Poor little goat," I said. "Slow down a bit. You're almost fat enough to eat now." This was in spite of the fact that the vegetable man had told me that the kid was far too fine a garbage can to be made into stew. Today my familiar world seemed a sad and savage place. Halfway down the hill I turned left, zigzagging through tiny streets with imaginative names — Kuche Yek, Kuche Do (Little Street One, Little Street Two). Tehran was full of these, which was one reason it was just as well not to have home mail delivery. One half of my mind was thinking about all these trivial things while the other half seemed to have died, and my feet were taking me closer and closer to the center of Tajrish.

When I reached the entrance to the bazaar I stopped. Maybe it's still there, I said to myself, and then, So what if it is? Did I come all the way down here just to look at some stupid graffiti? There were not many unbroken walls in the bazaar, and the logical one was close to hand. I swerved around the entrail vendor, who seemed to be offering me a still quivering heart in a piece of newspaper, and turned down the dim passageway. There it was, just as I had suspected, the tall, white Arabic script showing up clearly in the gloom. There were three contributions, but the only writing I recognized was Shaheen's — bold, elegant, unmistakable. I stared at it for a moment and then turned and went out again into the sunlight, past the shining mounds of fruit and around the corner into Old Shemiran Road. In five minutes I was standing in front of the Tajrish police station wondering what I was going to say to the young policeman who was lounging at the door.

He straightened and fixed his attention on the vee of my shirt. "May I help you?" he said in English.

"I don't think so," I answered dubiously.

His smile broadened. "May I fuck you?" he inquired, still in the same tea-party accents.

I had been propositioned before in Iran but never with quite such mind-boggling aplomb. It shook me out of my bemused state. "I applaud the elegance of your language, but no thank you just the same," I said, and was rewarded with a look of total confusion. Having exhausted his supply of English, he next made a suggestion in Farsi which was, if possible, even more explicit than the first. I was by now extremely angry, and perhaps I have that loutish cop to thank for the adrenalin which carried me on into the Tajrish police station. "Get out of my way, you of the burnt father. I have come to see your captain," I shouted and stormed through the door, leaving him to protest feebly on the steps.

I found myself in a sort of entrance hall, and there I stopped, wondering what to do next. All my senses were sharpened by fear so that I was aware of the most trivial details. It was a curiously homey, shabby place with several closed doors and a stairway leading up on one side. No one seemed to be about, but after a moment I began to distinguish voices behind the doors. What sounded like a number of small but impassioned domestic dramas were being played out in every corner of the building. From one direction came the voices of a husband and wife berating each other. This was overlaid by a loud voice complaining of a neighbor's noisiness and an equally loud voice denying the charge. Other, less distinguishable quarrels were going on at the same time in the background. Where, I wondered, were the police? Was there an officer closeted with each embattled party patiently waiting to get a word in edgewise? And where in this strange but somehow not very threatening building was Shaheen? I was rapidly losing my nerve when a slim, impeccably uniformed officer came down the stairs and stopped in front of me with a quizzical expression on his classically handsome face.

"May I be of service to you, mademoiselle?" he asked in the most English of English.

I said the first thing that came into my head, "I want to make a complaint about the arrest of a friend. Your officers arrested a friend of mine by mistake."

The straight, black eyebrows rose a fraction of an inch. "Indeed?" he said. "I am sure if they had known, they would have refrained."

This was terrible. I had made a fool of myself and lost any tiny advantage I might have had. I felt myself turn red from head to foot and even, to my horror, a warning prickle in my eyes. Fortunately the hall was dim. "That is not what I meant," I said with as much dignity as I could muster. "I really do have a serious complaint, and I would be obliged if you or someone in authority would listen to it."

"I do apologize," he said dryly. "Please come to my office. I am Captain Shirazi. I will try to assist you."

"How do you do? Thank you." I said to his back as he turned and headed up the stairs.

Captain Shirazi's office was also rather the worse for wear, but it was quieter than the downstairs hall. A window gave onto a small, green courtyard, and across the way I could see a narrow balcony with a cage full of blue parakeets hanging from the railing. He gestured me to a chair and sat down himself behind a desk.

"Your full name, please, mademoiselle," he said, taking up a pen. His voice was as courteous as ever, but I felt a chill go up my spine. The comedy was over now, and I was face to face with real authority. I was here to save Shaheen, and the only way I was going to do that was to tell this highly intelligent police officer a story that was plausible enough to be believed. A lost cause if there ever was one.

I gave the captain my name and the names of my parents and our address and our nationality (just for the record). Then I stopped.

"And the name of the person whom you believe to have been falsely arrested?" he said, still in the same silky voice.

"Shaheen Rohani."

"Ah yes," he said. "Rohani," and he began to go through the papers on his desk with what struck me as ostentatious thoroughness. He's playing with me, I thought. He knew all along why I was here, and he certainly doesn't have to look for any dossier.

Captain Shirazi, however, seemed happy to find what he was looking for. He held up an alarmingly thick folder with a triumphant gesture. "Here we are at last," he cried jovially. "Shaheen Rohani. Now let us see what the trouble seems to be." He started to leaf through the contents of the folder,

227

and as he did so, his face darkened dramatically. I watched him, gathering my strength, thinking, Half of this is an act, and acting is a game two can play better than one. Come on, Jill. If he hadn't wanted to play this scene he would have thrown you out by now.

"Mademoiselle Alexander," he said at last, looking up from the folder and fixing me with a somber gaze, "I fear that it is you rather than the police who have been mistaken."

"Really?" I said. "How so?"

"This young man," he said, giving the papers a scornful flick with the end of a finger, "this Shaheen Rohani — is a well-known agitator, an advocate of the downfall of His Majesty Mohammad Reza Pahlavi, and an Islamic Marxist."

I laughed (a good piece of acting in itself). "This is certainly a case of mistaken identity then," I said. "The one I know, the one whom you have so shamefully arrested, is a talented musician and a serious student bound for university in the United States. I assure you he has no time for subversive activities, and as for being an Islamic Marxist, I never knew anyone who was less of either."

"I am afraid I must inform you," he said stiffly, "that this exemplary youth was apprehended last night in the act of writing inflammatory slogans on a wall of the bazaar."

"Not in the act," I said. "Let's be precise, captain."

"How do you know?" he shot back, and I saw my chance and pounced.

"Because I was there," I cried, "and Shaheen Rohani did not write one single word. The rest of us did — just for a thrill. He kept telling us not to but, of course, he was the one your dumb policemen had to catch."

He stared at me with unfeigned astonishment. "So," he

228

said, "a nice American girl, a guest in a foreign country, you spend your time writing filth on walls, just for a thrill as you say. I am appalled."

It was time to grovel a little. "I really apologize," I said humbly. "It was a stupid thing to do. Life gets boring sometimes. Please forgive me, captain."

He was smiling slightly now, and I wasn't sure I liked the look of it. "Are you then proficient in the Persian language?" he asked smoothly.

"Not too bad," I said.

"You read and write Farsi?"

I nodded, praying silently that he wouldn't put me to any too revealing test.

"Excellent!" he cried. "Then, perhaps you will demonstrate your slogan-writing abilities on that blackboard over there."

I turned my head and saw the blackboard for the first time. It seemed like a funny thing for a police captain to have, but it would serve my purpose admirably.

"Delighted," I said, and jumping to my feet, I seized a new white chalk and swiftly, before my nerve could fail, I slashed Shaheen's banal message in bold Arabic characters on the board. It was by no means a perfect job, but I knew his writing and had seen it only minutes ago on the wall in the bazaar. Given the difference in surface and writing tools, it was plenty good enough. I turned smiling toward my adversary who was leaning back in his chair regarding me with an enigmatic expression. For what seemed like an eternity we just looked at each other. Then he leaned forward and pushed a buzzer on his desk. "What a remarkable young woman you are," he said softly. "I doubt very much if Shaheen Rohani deserves such loyalty."

"He does," I cried passionately. "You don't know him."

"Perhaps not," he said. "Perhaps I should avail myself of this opportunity."

The door opened and a policeman came in. "Bring Rohani," Captain Shirazi said, and the man left. I stood rooted by the blackboard, the chalk still in my hand, my heart beating wildly. Whether I had won or lost, the suspense would soon be over. Even the captain, who was still relaxed behind his desk, smiling cynically, must be ready to end our little drama.

In less than a minute the door opened again and Shaheen was there with the policeman behind him. He was handcuffed but seemed otherwise unharmed. When he saw me, what little color had been in his face drained away, and I wondered which one of us was the more likely to faint.

"Take those things off," Shirazi barked in Farsi, and when the guard had complied, he went on in English. "Well, Rohani," he said, "it would seem that a mistake has been made."

Shaheen had now taken in the message on the blackboard, and his eyes widened.

"This fool of a girl," the captain went on, "has been good enough to demonstrate to my satisfaction the authorship of the graffiti, and since this is the crime for which you were being held, I am forced to release you. I should hold her instead, but being lazy and corrupt like all the Iranian police . . ." (Here he paused for our reaction but got nothing except two mesmerized stares.) "Being, as I said, a lazy man," he went on, "I do not wish to spend my days wrangling with the American consul, so I will let her go. I hope you both understand that this ridiculously benign action in no way condones any of your activities and that you will be

230

from now on under constant surveillance. Do not step out of bounds again," he finished, staring straight at Shaheen.

"No, sir," Shaheen said.

I, however, felt that something more was called for. I advanced upon Captain Shirazi, and he rose from his desk. "Captain," I said, "I want to thank you for the courtesy and intelligence with which you have handled this case," and I held out my hand. For a long moment he stared thoughtfully into my eyes. Then, once more the inscrutable sophisticate, he kissed my extended fingers. "My pleasure, mademoiselle," he said.

Before we got into the car, I went to a public phone and called my home. So little time had elapsed that Dad had not even called. "If you hear from him," I said to my mystified mother, "tell him the problem has been solved and that tonight I will a tale unfold." It was all I could do. I hoped that he would telephone before trying to round up any influential friends.

The MG stood like a small green beetle at the far end of the bazaar parking lot — a welcome sight, friendly and familiar. Once in my usual place beside Shaheen I began to tremble from head to foot. He put his hand on my arm and looked at me with grave, astonished eyes. "How did you ever think up a mad scheme like that, much less carry it out?" he asked.

I shook my head. "I didn't think," I said. "If I had thought, I'd still be pacing the floor at home, and you would still be in that awful place. Oh Shaheen, when I saw you in handcuffs, I thought I would die."

"Don't think about it," he said. "I was lucky."

"Lucky!" I said indignantly, and he laughed.

"Lucky enough to have a crazy girl friend," he said. "I

suppose the captain is a secret sympathizer with the revolution. One finds them in strange places."

"I think it was more likely my feminine charms," I said, and had the satisfaction of seeing a look of alarm cross his face. "Don't worry," I added. "There was hardly time for a big seduction scene, and I don't suppose we will ever know what really went on inside his head. The lucky thing was finding a civilized policeman to deal with."

"Civilized and dangerous," Shaheen said. "That man was capable of anything. You took a fearful chance, Jill."

"Well," I said, "it's over now. Must we go to school, do you think?"

"God no. Mr. Perenyi will have a stroke, but no." He peered down at my feet and saw that I had sneakers on.

"Yes," I said, reading his mind, "let's go to the mountains, but aren't you tired? You must have been up all night."

"I feel like new," Shaheen said, and turned the car up toward Darband.

Chapter 33

So we climbed for the last time into the hills above Tehran. White thunderheads were gathering in the high passes, but we ignored their threat, grateful that more prudent hikers would see them and stay home. On a spur below Pas Qaleh we turned and looked back over the city, its haze broken here and there by dark columns of smoke. I shivered slightly as I looked, and Shaheen said, "What is it, Jill? What's frightening you?"

"That battlefield out there," I said. "That huge city that has only just begun to burn. Come to America with me, Shaheen. I don't want to think of you out there."

He tightened his grip on my hand but continued to gaze out over the smoking city. At last he said, "You don't know how much I long to leave. I have dreams of college in America — probably not very accurate, but you know how it is with dreams. One fixes on a scene and plays it over and over again." I nodded, and he went on. "It is always the fall of the year — cool and crisp, the air very clear. The big trees on the campus have turned to wonderful colors, and I am walking under them toward a white concert hall where I will hear some great musician play." He turned and smiled at me. "Have I got even part of it right?"

"You've got all of it right," I said. "It could be any New England campus in the fall." My eyes had filled with tears, and he put his arm around me, turning me away from the view over Tehran.

"Enough of that," he said. "This was meant to be a celebration, not a wake, so let's go find a patch of grass and do some celebrating before it rains."

We turned on the path below Pas Qaleh and found an orchard which had run wild, the old trees tangled and unpruned but still green from the water of a mountain stream. The grass was thick around their roots, and all mankind seemed very far away.

Shaheen had, not for the first time, brought the old blanket from the car. This we spread ceremoniously beneath a tree and sank upon it in each other's arms.

(They say the first time that a girl makes love is rarely a success. This may be true; I think it is, but not for me. Sometimes, indeed, I wish my body could forget the passion and fulfillment of that afternoon. Then I could sleep well at night and not wake shuddering with desire. And yet I know that I would not trade one moment of our love for fifty years of peaceful slumbering.)

Time passed unmarked by us until the wind began to rise. I felt its cool touch on my bare back and raised my head, seeing the patterns of dappled light shift on the long body at my side. He was at least half asleep. "Shaheen," I said, "I think it's going to pour."

Black eyes opened and smiled up at me. "Let it pour," he said. "We'll lie on our clothes and keep them dry."

"But parts of us may freeze."

234

"I'll lie on you, too," he volunteered, and pulled me down again.

Soon it grew clear that love was not going to be enough shelter from the elements. The sky darkened alarmingly while the wind began to tear through the gnarled branches of our tree. We put ourselves together hastily and made a dash for the trail. The storm pursued us down the mountainside but did not break until we were almost to the car. Even so we were as wet as if a small lake had risen up and dropped on us by the time we had scrambled, laughing wildly, into our seats.

"We'll drown the poor little thing," I said, as water cascaded off me onto the floor.

"Nonsense. This car is English," Shaheen said proudly.

"But in England the rain patters down. It doesn't fall all in one gigantic drop." I gathered my hair in one hand and wrung it out as far from the dashboard as I could get.

"You'll see — if I don't electrocute myself," Shaheen said, reaching gingerly for the ignition; and the faithful little motor gave its accustomed throaty roar.

My father, looking less ravaged but a good deal more confused, met us just inside the door. He looked us up and down. "Persian water torture?" he said at last.

"Something like that," Shaheen replied. And then, to my astonishment, the two men embraced, the older just a shade awkwardly, the younger with the easy warmth that was common among his countrymen. I stood watching them, more touched by far than if I had been the object of this display.

We spent the next hours getting dry without and wet within from an amazingly large but ill-assorted hoard of alcoholic odds and ends. My mother, after hearing a somewhat censored version of the day's events, retired to the kitchen with a purposeful stride. There, out of leftovers even more curious than the drinks, she produced a meal which to our impaired faculties seemed fit for kings. It was a splendid evening, brief but bright — unmarred by the shadow of future grief. Finally, however, food, drink, sex, rain, and release from an enormous fear all in one day had their inevitable effect. Shaheen sat down on the couch after dinner and fell asleep in the middle of a sentence. My parents stretched him out right where he was and covered him with an extra blanket. "I feel as if I had acquired a third child," my mother said, and then fled sniffling to the bedroom wing. Too tired for more emotion, I followed her and dropped on my bed like a stone.

Chapter 34

Contrary to what one might expect, Sha-
heen and I played well the following night. We played, in
fact, far beyond our ordinary powers.

For once, I was not even particularly nervous, only strung
to a high pitch of concentration and intensity. We delivered
the obligatory marches with aplomb, and the sentimental
suite for band on a theme of MacDowell, and the cute piece
full of little jokes for woodwinds and snare drums. It was all
very well done, and the audience of parents applauded du-
tifully. Then came a longer pause while the wind players
rubbed their lips gently and prayed for strength. Mr. Perenyi
stood before us with his head bowed, turning the white baton in his slender hands. Then he straightened and swept us
with a smile of such confidence and warmth that I felt a
surge of triumph before we had even begun to play. He
raised his hands; the murmur of the audience died away; and
the deep, sonorous voice of Beethoven filled the auditorium.

I felt my optimism grow as the overture progressed from
those first, somber chords through the soaring lyricism of the
middle section. Shaheen and I were playing as if but one
breath and one will poured through the shining coils of our

instruments, underlining the melodies with soft pencil strokes of sound, deepening the richness behind the other voices. The tempo increased, and we urged it onward with stinging offbeats. From time to time he glanced at me with a slight smile, and I returned his look, feeling each time a new wave of joy. Then came that moment when all four horns spoke together out of the silence — the perfect, close chord ringing forth in the dark hall. I saw our conductor's eyes widen. For a moment I thought he was going to raise a hand to hold us down, but he smiled and, at the next entrance, beckoned us on to greater heights. The tempestuous finale was a trial of strength, which, for the first time, we passed triumphantly. When the last echoes had died away, we stood breathless and amazed, listening to the audience applaud.

To my surprise and, I think, to Shaheen's, Agha Rohani was among the parents milling around in the auditorium after the concert. We found him shaking hands with my father, who was looking more enormous and, in spite of his best efforts, more rumpled than usual next to the sartorial splendor of the carpet king. He clapped his son on the back, kissed my hand, and made all the appropriate noises about our marvelous horn playing. Then he turned back to my parents. "I brought a good-sized car and a bottle of rather respectable champagne," he said. "Let me drive you home, and we will drink a toast to our young musicians. What do you say?"

My mother was looking starry-eyed, partly perhaps with emotion over our playing, but she was also far from immune to the charms of Agha Rohani. "That's the nicest thing anyone has proposed to me in a long time," she said.

Shaheen shrugged. We had, of course, been looking forward to the drive back alone. "Just so we get the back seat," he said. "We need the space for our horns."

"I think the rest of us can manage to squeeze into the front," his father answered dryly, "and I would hate to think of your horns rattling around forlornly in the boot. Come on. We'll give it a try."

The "good-sized car" turned out to be a Mercedes of heroic proportions. Shaheen and I fitted ourselves into about one quarter of the back seat and left the rest to our instruments. We held each other as the great car slid through the dark city, feeling the familiar turns and the soft surge of speed as it devoured the open road over the dunes. "I think I'll get a chauffeur," he mumbled into my ear. "This beats driving, but then I'll always need a beautiful woman to hold in the back seat."

I burrowed deeper into his shoulder. "I'll stay right here," I said. "Someone can feed me through the window." It was one of those journeys you wish would never end, but there was little traffic to slow us down, and soon we felt the last sharp turn and heard the deepened growl of the motor as we took the steep slope of Asef.

Champagne, toasts, laughter. It turned out that there were two bottles, not one, and they were very respectable indeed and very cold, having reposed in a large tub of ice in the trunk of the car during the concert. I wondered if Shaheen's father had heard about the incident with the police and if this was his way of thanking us. As it happened, I was only partly right.

We finished the champagne, and Agha Rohani got up as if to go. Instead he walked to the window and stood looking up toward the light that shines like a star on the flank of the mountain range marking the top of the trail from Niavarin. "I used to go up there often," he said, turning back to us with a face that was suddenly, unaccountably sad. "I suppose you two have made that climb?

He seemed to be speaking to me more than anyone, and I nodded, smiling but uncertain what to say. Then he strode toward us, taking an envelope from the breast pocket of his linen suit, laying it abruptly on the coffee table in front of Dad. "Well," he said, "the champagne was for our mutual joy, but this, I fear, you really need."

Slowly my father reached out, and I saw his face change as he opened the envelope. He held the contents up for us to see. "Four tickets to New York," he said, "dated three days from now."

"I had hoped to find a client for your so useful skills," Rohani went on before we could react, "but, as you know, it is not my field, and Iran is not the place it was even a few years ago. No one now wants to move ahead or think new thoughts. The marriage of Iran and the West which once seemed so promising is almost at an end. So this is the best that I can do."

My father stood holding the tickets spread out like a fan, and I thought his hand trembled a little. "I can't let you do this," he said, and we were all uncomfortably aware that he was holding the equivalent of about four thousand dollars in his hand.

The carpet merchant, however, had recovered his relaxed and urbane manner. "My dear friend, don't give it a thought," he said. "There are all kinds of ways and means, trade-offs, favors. You must study the bazaar some day in more settled times." He turned, sparkling, to me. "Perhaps I have unloaded the white elephant of Kurdistan at last. Who knows? With a little attention to detail, everything works out to everyone's mutual advantage. By the way, I will send someone for this improbable purple affair tomorrow. Much as I would like you to have it, you wouldn't be able to carry it on the plane, and I would hate to think of your fat friend upstairs taking it for back rent."

He was chattering — giving us time to adjust to the implications of his gift. Shaheen and I stared at each other, numb with shock. We had all grown used to living from day to day as if the more distant future did not exist. I turned and glanced quickly at my mother and then away, certain that she was about to cry. It was a fine way to respond to such a princely offer, but I knew Agha Rohani understood our conflicting emotions. He turned to my father, who was still trying to find something to say, and said gently, "You know, the oil company might let you starve for months, and getting into really bad trouble with debts sometimes does make it difficult to leave Iran. Much better to go now and hope to come back in more propitious days."

Dad found his voice at last and held out his hand. "You're absolutely right," he said. "I know it even if my sentimental family doesn't seem to have grasped the facts of life. We are all more grateful than I can say. Please believe me."

The other man gripped his hand — a terse, British handshake. "I do," he said briefly. "Come, Shaheen."

Shaheen rose as if in a dream and started for the door. "I'll call you, Jill," was all he managed to say.

Agha Rohani turned to us one last time with eyes which I was amazed to see were full of tears. "*Khoda hafez*, dear American friends," he said. "Go with God." And then they were gone.

Chapter 35

*The next three days were hectic and pain-*ful in about equal proportions. We found that there was an incredible amount of work to do and that we had accumulated many more possessions than we had thought. The size of the house and our lack of furniture had given a deceptively spartan impression even to us, but when closets and cupboards were turned out, we were appalled by the year's acquisitions. We would have no time for the usual departing foreigners' sale. The Enrights, however, had agreed to keep the things which were either too valuable or too well loved to throw away. Some boxes we labeled "sell this, if you can," and others would be included in their shipment when they, too, left Iran. Altogether it was an enormous amount of work, but I highly recommend the job of moving in too short a time as therapy for the broken-hearted.

I did not go back to Community School, even to say good-bye to my friends or teachers, but Mr. Perenyi called me one night. He had a lot to say about my horn playing and about the absurdity of my college plans, which at that time ran to things like English literature. I listened and mumbled my thanks. "But it's Shaheen you should be worried about," I said finally.

"What the hell can I do with him?" the conductor shouted. "Does he listen to you when you tell him not to throw his life away? Of course not. And now he thinks I am some kind of revolutionary hero. All I want is for him to get out of here and play the horn, but what can I do?"

"I don't know," I said, "but try, Mr. Perenyi. Maybe he'll listen to you. And thanks for everything."

Shaheen, too, had stayed out of school to help us pack. It was good to have him there beside me as I rummaged and sorted, and from time to time we even recovered some of our old gaiety as we unearthed an odd souvenir or leafed through my brother's drawings. James, having little enthusiasm for packing, was spending these last days in school, and the chance to see some of the sketches he had done of family and friends was too good to miss. There was even one of the MG which showed through the windshield tiny portraits of Shaheen and me crouched under a surrealistic tangle of French horn tubing.

Ali, of course, was nearly useless, except to clean up after our meager meals, and the sight of his despairing face was a constant reminder, if any were needed, of our own sorrow. Still, I thought, parting from Ali and putting his miseries behind us could be counted on a rather short list of present blessings. My mother found him touching, and perhaps he was. Certainly it became clear that he was a lot more fond of us than we had ever suspected. My parents, he said, had become his parents and James his little brother. I imagine his feelings toward me remained ambiguous to the end.

The final day arrived. We were to fly in the afternoon, and

that morning Shaheen brought the big Mercedes to take the boxes down to the Enrights' house. The sun was hot as we loaded the car, and we were too tired and out of sorts to deal very well with Barbara's tearful farewells or her mother's attempt to comfort us with Oreos. Still it had to be done. The Enrights had been kind, I reminded myself, and our things were going to be a nuisance in their overfurnished house. We made our escape as politely as possible and started back through the little streets where James and I had run our sled on a night that already seemed a thousand years ago. "I'm not going to take you to the airport," Shaheen said suddenly. "Coward that I am, I can't take that scene."

"I know," I said. "There's nothing worse."

"I've ordered a cab," he went on. "The driver is a friend of mine. It won't cost anything."

"Come on, Shaheen. We still have a few rials left," I said.

"Use them to buy drinks on the plane. Knock yourself out and sleep all the way home."

"It sounds more like a recipe for instant tears," I said, "but what the hell? I'm tired of being a heroine."

Shaheen gave me a somber smile and turned his attention back to the road. We were nosing slowly along a narrow street between two high walls. Great poplars rose up behind them into the painfully blue sky. I thought he was looking for a place to park where we could be alone, but, as always, this seemed to be a futile task. "Do you think we have time to go up to Vallenjak?" he asked.

I shook my head. "Mum would have a collapse if we didn't come back soon."

"Dogged to the end by family, friends, and the general public," he said bitterly and stepped on the accelerator.

In the last hour before the cab came to take us to the

plane, Shaheen and I walked in the garden holding hands. The first roses were in bloom, and the pansies of No Ruz spilled over the edges of the empty swimming pool. We said the usual things with lengthy pauses in between. We said that we would write, that he would come soon, or that I would soon return. At last Shaheen stopped with his back to the house and took a small box out of his pocket. "I gave this a lot of thought," he said, handing it to me. Inside was a bracelet of exquisite Iranian workmanship. The thin, gold circle was perfectly plain, but the clasp was a *simurgh* with outstretched wings and tiny, emerald eyes. I stood speechless while he fastened it around my wrist. "Naturally," he said, "I thought of a ring, but I didn't want you to feel . . ." He paused and raised his head. For a moment we looked into each other's eyes.

"Constrained?" I said, and he nodded silently. I touched the little, shining creature with one finger. "I shall wear it like a ring," I told him. "Exactly like a ring, Shaheen."

From the other side of the house we heard the taxi blow its horn, the front door slam, my father's shout; and we had time for only one fierce kiss.

It is late August now, and soon we must leave this haven by the sea. My parents and James are off to a job in Mexico, but my days of wandering are over for a while; I should have practiced more and written less this summer since I am entering Juilliard in the fall. So much for English lit.

The light of morning slants across my desk, kindling the green eyes of the Persian phoenix on my wrist. Now I feel drained but strangely free, and some of the pain has flowed from me into this great mound of words.

Still, before picking up the horn, I'll walk to town. The

sun is strong today; the shadows of the rocks are sharp and black. But for the endless murmur of the sea, I could almost be on some desolate ridge above Tehran. Perhaps he is walking out, I think, leaving Iran on foot through the mountains of Turkestan. This could take months, I tell myself, as I follow the well-worn path out over the cliffs to check the mail.